D1137797

The Player was Michael Tolkin's first novel, and he adapted the book for the screen. The movie, which he co-produced, was directed by Robert Altman. In 1991 Tolkin wrote and directed his first feature, *The Rapture*. His second novel, *Among the Dead*, will be published in 1993.

ff

THE
PLAYER

Michael Tolkin

faber and faber
LONDON · BOSTON

First published in the USA,
and simultaneously in Canada, in 1988
by The Atlantic Monthly Press, New York
First published in Great Britain in 1988 by
Faber and Faber Limited
3 Queen Square London WC1N 3AU
This paperback edition first published in 1989

Printed in England by Clays Ltd, St Ives plc

A CIP record for this book is
available from the British Library

ISBN 0-571-15397-6

4 6 8 10 9 7 5 3

This book was written with the good counsel
of
Wendy Mogel and Louis Breger

This book is dedicated
to
Horace Beck and Olga Smyth,
two fine teachers

The witch that came (the withered hag)
To wash the steps with pail and rag
Was once the beauty Abishag,

The picture pride of Hollywood.
Too many fall from great and good
For you to doubt the likelihood.

Die early and avoid the fate.
Or if predestined to die late,
Make up your mind to die in state.

Make the whole stock exchange your own!
If need be occupy a throne,
Where nobody can call you crone.

Some have relied on what they knew,
Others on being simply true.
What worked for them might work for you.

No memory of having starred
Atones for later disregard
Or keeps the end from being hard.

Better to go down dignified
With boughten friendship at your side
Than none at all. Provide, provide!

—Robert Frost,
"Provide, Provide"

Not you, lean quarterlies and swarthy periodicals
with your studious incursions toward the pomposity of ants,
nor you, experimental theatre in which Emotive Fruition
is wedding Poetic Insight perpetually, nor you,
promenading Grand Opera, obvious as an ear (though you
are close to my heart), but you, Motion Picture Industry
it's you I love!

In times of crisis, we must all decide again and again whom we love.

—Frank O'Hara,
"To the Film Industry in Crisis"

CHAPTER ONE

Just as Griffin suspected, there was a meeting in Levison's office without him. From the path outside the administration building he could see the back of Levison's couch on the second floor. Was the meeting over? Levison was shaking hands with someone; Griffin couldn't see who it was. He knew he was watching the end of his job. He debated whether he should go to his office or return to the screening room he'd just left. He could use the phone there to call Jan, his secretary, for messages. If he went straight to his office, he would pass Levison's, and he didn't want Celia, Levison's secretary, to see him in this moment of shame. Well it is shame, he thought.

He stared at the notebook in his hands and hated Levison for putting it there. Levison had asked him to watch the directing debut of a British producer, an old friend. And out of respect for Levison and his friendships, Griffin had made a careful assessment of the film, since Levison said he hadn't time to see it before a meeting with the director. Did Levison really care about the film or his old friend? Not enough to screen the thing for himself. Twenty-one minutes into the movie, Griffin could have stopped it, because not enough had happened. He had stayed in the screening room to hide, because he knew that Levison needed him, literally, in the dark for a few hours. Griffin was used to hiding at the right moment. Once he had gone to Paris to hide, when a film he had supervised was coming out. The film was terrible, and he wanted to avoid the blame. That was only last year, when he had been heir apparent. Everyone thought Levison was finished, but Levison held on.

He went back to the screening room. When he opened the door, he saw the production staff of a television show about to watch the film they had shot the day before. He didn't know anyone's name, but they all knew his. He apologized for interrupting them, someone asked if he wanted to stay. It was a transparent flattery, and he closed the door. The room across the hall was empty. He called Jan.

"Griffin Mill's office."

"It's me." He sounded weak, something caught in his throat.

"You got another postcard. Maybe I should call Walter Stuckel." Stuckel was head of studio security.

"What does this one say?"

He waited while Jan went through the pile of mail on her desk. "It says, 'You said you'd get back to me. I'm still waiting.'"

"What's the picture?"

"It's a joke card. There's a wagon pulled by mules, and in the wagon there's this huge watermelon. It's some kind of a trick picture. It says, 'We grow 'em big in Texas.' Come on, Griffin, let me call Walter."

"No. A watermelon? I think I know who it is."

"Tell me."

"If I tell you, you'll tell Celia, and then everyone will know."

"So what, whoever it is who sends these cards looks like the jerk, not you."

"Trust me, it's contagious."

"What is, looking like a fool?"

"Yes. Besides, I know who it is, it's either Aaron Jonas or Steve Baylen, probably Baylen."

"No," said Jan, "I don't think the cards are coming from an agent, I think your secret correspondent is a writer. If you ask me."

Griffin knew it was a writer. The cards began about four weeks ago, a few a week, and yesterday, one of them appeared in his mailbox at home. It was in his pocket now. He supposed he had been followed home. Friends have my address, he thought, but this isn't from a friend. Why hadn't he called Walter Stuckel? Why was he so scared of him?

"Jan, trust me, this is some jerk friend of mine playing a stupid game. Let's change the subject. Any calls?"

"There's a meeting of all the department heads in Levison's office. You weren't invited."

"That's not a call."

"I thought you should know."

"Am I out?"

"Who knows?"

They said good-bye.

It was March, and when Griffin stepped out of the editors' building, the streets between the soundstages were empty. He wasn't sure why, but the idea that in this stillness lay all that was Hollywood excited him; he was almost embarrassed by this excitement over nothing, because there were no hordes of Indians and armies of Napoleon wandering around the lot, there was no sense of activity. Almost everyone said they hated the harsh yellow light that bounced off the high walls of the stages, but Griffin was not depressed by this calm. He liked the way he always separated into parts in the worst of the midday sun. It reminded him of marijuana, the pleasant terror of getting stoned in the middle of the day, of marching in step with the significance of things. Hot bright noons in Burbank were a kind of cosmic experience for him, because they were pointless, because the only tonic for the light, which was, in some sense, redemption's gleam, was money, work, authority. In what sense? he asked himself. In the sense that if Judgment Day is the only reason for conscience, then the bad feeling stirred by the light is an echo of some ultimate regret.

Now he was mad at this writer who had been sending him postcards. He took yesterday's card from his pocket. Paris Nightlife, the Eiffel Tower surrounded by cameos showing the Moulin Rouge, a fountain, Notre Dame. And the message. Typed, so the thin plastic coating of the card was broken, rippled: "You said you'd get back to me. We had a meeting, I told you my idea, you said you wanted to think about it, and you said that you'd get back to me. Well?"

The first postcard had come with a short message: "You said you'd get back to me." The handwriting was even, the letters a bit high and slanted but not eccentric, they were carefully spaced; it was like the impersonally romantic script of a love letter seen close-up in a movie. The postcard was probably from the early 1950s, a woman on the beach in Fort Lauderdale, under a bright orange umbrella. She wore extravagant sunglasses and a tortured smile. Griffin thought she would be happy that a Hollywood bigwig was finally looking at her. A few days later another postcard arrived, a glossy shot of the Eiffel Tower. The message was, "I'm waiting for your call." The day after that the third card came, with only one word. "Well?" The card was a picture of THE LATEST ADDITION TO UNITED'S FRIENDSHIP FLEET, a shortened version of the Boeing 747.

After that there were three more postcards, and none of them carried a message.

Across the street, he saw Mary Netter and Drew Posner, from Marketing. He braced himself for their buoyant onslaught. Drew waved his hand like the kid in fifth grade who has the answer all the time.

"Hey, Mister Vice-president," he said. Griffin tapped an invisible hat brim.

"So cool," said Mary. Mary had short hair; a month ago it had been a crew cut. Once, at a party, Drew asked Griffin if he'd like to rub his dick over Mary's head. Mary's laughter had embarrassed Griffin, and he felt that embarrassment as proof of something bad about himself, an inability to play.

Levison's meeting was over, Griffin could see the back of the empty sofa by the window. He took the long way around the building to his office, to avoid passing Celia. The end of his job was inevitable. There would be other work, other studios, but the glow around him was probably lost, and he would never be the head of production, not for a major studio, not for this studio or Universal or Disney or Columbia or Paramount or 20th-Century Fox. These were the last studios with property, with soundstages and back lots, where you could point to a building and say, "That was Alan Ladd's dressing room" or "Over there we made *Bringing Up Baby*." And if it was sentimental of him to get a little pleasure out of the history of these buildings, did that harm anyone? If the Writer knew he had held on for this last bad year with Levison because he didn't want to leave the lot would he like Griffin a little, see him as just another human being with the full assembly of reasons to be unhappy? Would the Writer understand that even if Griffin were offered a great job as head of a company with offices in a tall building in Century

City or Beverly Hills he might not want it, that the thought made him miserable? Orion and Tri-Star, big companies, were in office buildings, what difference did it make where they were? It just mattered to him, and he couldn't resist the gloom that soon he would have to give up a real studio with a real gate, trade in a parking space with his name painted on a concrete bumper for a pass to an underground garage. He wanted to say, how can you make a movie in an office building? That was another sentimental thought, but he caught himself and resisted the attack. Maybe he wasn't really sentimental enough. Wouldn't the studio's films have done better if he were more sentimental? Here he was, the centipede who tries to understand his own method, a sure way to stumble.

None of this was a surprise. For a few months Griffin had felt a slight change in the number of calls Jan logged during the day. One afternoon while she was away from her desk, Griffin had opened her files and compared a few days of recent phone logs with the logs from the year before. A year ago in three days Griffin had received two hundred and ninety-five. In the last three days he had received two hundred and eleven. He hadn't counted the calls by category, but it looked at a few glances as though agents trying to sell him screenplays and directors were not calling him as often. He had no trouble getting calls returned, but something in the wind was telling people that Griffin Mill was not the best first choice anymore. Could the Writer sending him the postcards understand that they were in the same business, with the same rules for everyone?

When he walked into his office, Jan tickled the air in front of her, grinning. There was a postcard propped against her typewriter. HOLLYWOOD AT NIGHT, THREE VIEWS OF THE GLAMOUR CAPITAL OF THE WORLD.

"It went to Accounting by accident, they just sent it over. Look on the back."

"No."

"Come on, it's a girl who's sending you these cards, it has to be."

Griffin picked the card up and turned it over. The message: "Is it me, or is it you?"

"You were at a party," said Jan, "and you told some girl you'd make her a star, and she went to bed with you. You said you'd call her and you never did. You flashed her that big lover-boy smile of yours and you caught her on it."

"I don't have to lie to women."

"Honey, all men lie to women. It's in the blood."

Griffin had an instant of clarity, and he smiled, he relaxed, he leaned forward, he brought his face near Jan's, he liked himself for the first time in weeks. "You got me," he said. "It doesn't happen often. You know as a rule I don't mess with actresses."

"But they have such nice legs."

"I'll tell you the truth, it's not the length, it's the way they feel. It's the skin. It's how they get to be stars, too, it's something about the way they radiate. I'll tell you what happened. There was a party, I wasn't drunk, but she was. She told me to take her home. I took her home. I stayed a few hours. It was fun."

"And now she wants you to make her a star. Except you don't even remember her name. So you caught her on your smile. I hope she knows it's like your car, that you have to give it back when you're fired."

Griffin let the line pass, but he saw in Jan's eyes that she wished she hadn't said it. He pressed ahead with the story. "Are you ready for the punch line? She *is* a star. She's a television star, and she wants to make it in the movies. And she knows she never will, but she wants to try. And she thought I could help her."

"So why doesn't she sign her name? Maybe you're lying right now. Maybe she isn't a television star. How would you know, you don't watch television. You're ashamed to admit a one-night stand with a girl whose name you can't remember."

"Maybe she isn't a star?" Griffin said, trying to slump in defeat. Then he came back on the attack. "But you know why she won't sign? She's trying to be original. She thinks, of course I remember her, everyone else does. She didn't sign the postcards the way bad writers who don't have agents draw cartoons and write jokes on the envelopes of screenplays they send in to famous directors. They draw big noses sticking out of the flaps and stars around the directors' names. They think that if they can't be good, at least they can be different. They go to novelty shops that print YOUR NAME HERE on the headlines of phony front pages and send these stupid things as cover letters with their scripts. The headline says, STEVEN SPIELBERG WINS OSCAR FOR DIRECTING YOUR-NAME-HERE'S STUPID SCREENPLAY.''

"It doesn't say 'stupid' on the headline."

"It doesn't have to."

"She's got to sign her name one of these days. Maybe she'll call you. Would you see her again?"

"I'll do what you tell me to do."

"Griffin, if she calls, or if you remember her name, or if she signs her name, be nice to her. If you use the casting couch, pay your debts."

"You'll be the first to know."

"The second," she said. She had closed the case.

Griffin's indignation developed a life of its own, and it remembered a party, an actress's long hair, kisses, promises. At dinner that night with Dick Mellen, his lawyer, Griffin heard himself babbling on about the postcards and the actress. Mellen, sixty-five, silver-haired, with a tan like brushed gold, had known Bogart, he had been drunk with Bogart a dozen times, which was why Griffin had hired him. Mellen didn't care about the cards.

"Put her in a movie," he said.

"But what if she can't act?" Griffin was surprised and annoyed with how shocked he sounded.

"That's what I'm telling you," said Mellen. "You know what they did in the old days? Prison movie. Visiting day. Long tracking shot down the room with all the little booths with the telephones. Wives and girlfriends, each one gets a close-up, each one the girlfriend of a different executive or producer."

"But she's the star of a television series."

"Which one?"

"I'm sworn not to say."

"Griffin, this isn't a joke."

"If she's any kind of grown-up, she'll keep it to herself."

"No. Grown-ups turn everything to their advantage and don't worry about scandal. At least they do in this town. If she's smart, her agent'll call Levison to talk about projects."

Griffin saw that he had lowered himself in Mellen's eyes, not for the actress but for making things inexcusably difficult.

Mellen changed the subject. "You know your job is not exactly secure right now."

"Everything will work out. We're making some good pictures." This was what he was supposed to say, and he didn't like the sound of it. The lie about the actress had upset his rhythm, he was measuring every thought now.

"I think they're bringing in Larry Levy."

Griffin exhaled, and with the rush of air again he tortured himself, this time for collapsing, for taking the news as a body blow, taking it badly. He always tried to contain the air, contain the feeling, not show too much excitement, not show unhappiness. This was the closest he came to meditation; when other executives whooped and slapped each other's palms if an audience cheered during the first sneak previews of a film, Griffin kept the feelings to himself. And now, instead of keeping the air inside, to stay firm, he was breaking one of his first rules. Without any control now he heard himself add another hatefully dull thought to the conversation. "Larry Levy's a jerk."

"Do you want to quit? I don't think you should."

"I'd like to run Columbia."

"You can't turn back the clock." The job had been offered a year ago, and Griffin had told them no. He had wanted Levison's job, and there was talk that he'd get it. The talk had been wrong.

"Keep your eyes open," said Griffin, another stupid phrase.

"That's what I do," said the lawyer.

Griffin wanted to tell Mellen that the story about the actress had been a lie, every word of it. If he told the truth, would the fissure between his thoughts and their expression be healed? Or was purification impossible without greater sacrifice and harder work?

A fresh thought came to him and made him sick. He would end up having to sell something, real estate or cars. If he lost his job during a round of musical chairs, he would be on the way to exile from Hollywood. This wouldn't happen immediately. The favors due him would be paid off, if he couldn't get important work at a big studio, one of the stars or directors he'd fought for might hire him to run his office and find material, and let him produce something if he'd been there from the beginning. If the films died, and the next crew of bright young executives saw him as a relic, then where could he go? Smaller companies, with little funding and few contacts. They would hire Griffin for his address book, not understanding that the book was as out of touch as the book's owner. Eventually, his disgrace would catch up with him, and everyone would know he was old, over the hill. One day he would be out of money. The next day he would put his house on the market, then take the profit and rent an apartment somewhere, and look for work outside of Hollywood, outside of the movies. By then he would be, what, forty? He tried to see himself at forty, selling German cars to young producers and studio executives. He imagined the ad in a newspaper, "Hi, I'm Griffin Mill, here to help put the entertainment professional behind the wheel of a precision motor car." Why not kill himself now? The fantasy ended with his funeral, and a crowd of pitying friends.

He didn't ask himself how he would come to die at forty. He would die of embarrassment. He chased these thoughts away, and tried to picture himself as an independent success, a real producer, a man of accomplishment, a man to be feared. Nothing. No such picture would emerge, there was too much interference from all the confusion in his life. He knew how anyone who had known him in the past would read the ad for the Mercedes dealership, "Hi, I'm Griffin Mill. I had promise, but I fucked myself."

Home in bed, Griffin looked through the dark to the postcard writer. He concentrated, trying to beam his mind to the Writer's mind, asking him to stop the cards. If the night is alive, thought Griffin, then what I tell the night in my room, the night can tell you in your room.

Leave me alone.

I'm sorry if I broke a promise. That's life.

Griffin saw these thoughts fall to the middle of the bed, dead. He pictured the distance between himself and the secret correspondent as a series of contiguous dark boxes, and he spoke aloud, testing the air with his voice and receiving a slight echo. "Hello? It's me, Griffin Mill. I said I'd get back to you. Well, here I am. Please stop sending the postcards. I can't stop thinking about them, and they're getting in my way. Listen, if I find out who you are before you identify yourself or stop sending these cards, you'll never work for me."

He thought the last part sounded stupid, and imagined an audience agreeing with him, saying, "Yes, Griffin, that pathetic threat sure is stupid." The sense of someone watching felt like a good sign, that he'd gotten through.

The next morning he had breakfast at the Polo Lounge with Levison. They met every Wednesday; it was so much a part of their schedules that they no longer confirmed the meeting unless it was going to be canceled.

"Read any good scripts lately?" asked Levison.

"*Chinatown*."

"They already made that one."

"I read it last week."

"You know they'd never make it now. They wouldn't even make *Saturday Night Fever* now."

Griffin smiled. "Excuse me, but you and I are 'they.'"

"I'm 'they.' You're almost 'they,' but not quite." Griffin didn't like Levison's curdled smile. The mild remark came quickly, and it seemed to Griffin that Levison regretted it. Levison continued, "In *Saturday Night Fever*, Travolta wins the dance contest but realizes it's a hollow victory, that the world of the discos is an empty world. Can you see that now?"

"He grows up in the story. What difference does the background make? Plus the music is great. And the dancing is great."

"Forget it, Griffin, the ending is ironic. The audience is too angry, too impatient. They hate ambiguity, they want everything reconciled."

"Why wasn't I at the meeting yesterday?" Attack.

"There may be some changes."

"Am I in or out?"

"Larry Levy is coming aboard." He said this quietly.

"I report to you. I'm not going through Levy. If I have to report to Levy, I quit."

"You can't quit. I won't let you, and you have a year and a half on your contract. I'll get in your way if you try. Don't go looking for offers at other studios. I'll hold you to your contract, and if you make trouble, I'll sue you for breach unless you come to the office every day, and I won't have anything for you to do. Relax. Levy's bright. He was available, and I thought we could use him. He's good. He's real good."

"I know him," said Griffin, irritated.

"He can make us all look good."

"So I'm not the flavor of the month anymore?"

"You haven't been for a year. And neither have I. And Larry Levy will lose his flavor too. Look, if you really want to leave, I won't stop you. I want you to stay. Griffin, I need you, but I can understand your feelings. Forget what I said about a lawsuit. If it's impossible to share the power, I'll give you a development deal. You can be a producer."

"Right, so *Variety* can quote me saying, 'It's a chance I've been waiting for since I came to Hollywood. I'm thrilled.'"

"Don't be bitter." Levison poured him another cup of coffee, which Griffin accepted against his will. The coffee burned his stomach all day and made him feel like he was gliding over the surface of everything, impossible to find traction.

At the office, Jan handed him a souvenir packet of "Ten Memories From Southern California," a pleated strip of cards that folded flat and then closed with a tab inserted through the card on the back. The front was for the address but managed to save room for a cartoon of the region, with the most famous sights drawn in extreme relief. Disneyland's Matterhorn was the size of Everest, huge surfers rode boards the size of aircraft carriers on tidal waves into Malibu. A camera on a tripod was the Colossus of Hollywood and Vine. The picture on the back was of

BEAUTIFUL LAKE ARROWHEAD, JUST AN HOUR FROM THE WORLD'S FINEST GOLFING AND SAILING. Griffin opened the packet. This message was typed.

> *Dear Griffin,*
>
> *I'm still waiting for you to call. You said you'd get back to me. My answering machine is on all the time, so you can't say that you called but I wasn't in. I told you my idea, you said you wanted to think about it, and you said you'd get back to me. My agent said that was a good sign, the part about getting back to me. I've waited long enough. You lied to me. It's obvious you have no intention of hiring me. In the name of all the writers in Hollywood who get pushed around by executives who know nothing more about movies than what did well last week and have no passion for film, I'm going to kill you.*

Griffin folded the cards.

"Well, who's it from?" asked Jan. "The actress?"

"She says she was just having fun with me and wants to know if I'll have dinner with her soon. She says she knows how hard it is to cross over from TV to film, but she wants to try, and she's not holding me to any drunken promises."

He danced to his office and pulled the door shut. He hoped that he was smiling.

Why aren't I afraid? he asked himself. Why don't I call Walter Stuckel? It would be so easy to show him the postcards. Griffin pictured himself withdrawing from Stuckel's concern; it would be that arm around his shoulder, an hour of advice about security, a bodyguard, an investigation into his friends. Word would get out that he was a target. Stigma.

He called Jan on the intercom. "I'm going to be tied up on the phone for a while. It's important. Tell anyone who wants me that I'll be back later." Then he called the number for the time, so a light on Jan's phone would show that he was talking, that he was busy. He took his desk calendar and sat on the couch. He got up quickly and went to his refrigerator for a can of tomato juice. He put the latest postcard on his coffee table and tried to take a deep breath. The room was quiet.

A few phrases leapt from the card, like the Southern California Hilites on the cover. *My idea . . . my agent . . . everyone knows . . . writers . . .*

Griffin turned the pages of the calendar. Three or four times a week he heard ideas from writers he didn't know. Most of them had never had a movie produced. Griffin barely remembered the names or the faces. He remembered none of the ideas more than two weeks old. He remembered enthusiasm, calculated optimism and offensive cheeriness, and sometimes a sad, embarrassing panic. Yesterday one had come in; Griffin had already forgotten his name and he checked it on the calendar. Doug Krieger. Doug Krieger, without saying hello, launched into the story from the effect of silence after the brilliant title sequence faded to the rhythm of a hundred drummers from Ghana. He was pitching some stupid African adventure story. No one would want to make it.

Griffin looked at the names of other writers. Jan never gave them longer than thirty minutes. He never needed more than fifteen. Some tried to condense their ideas to twenty-five words, in and out, as they'd learned in some screenwriting class taught by someone who'd made a science of yesterday's formula. They'd talk about the "arc of the story." They'd use little code words and phrases like *paradigm* and *first-act bump.* They were exact. "At minute twenty-three she finds out . . ." What does she find out? That this movie won't get made. They'd talk about "the rules of the genre." They'd set the scene with casting: Jeff Bridges and Meryl Streep are locked in a bank vault. They combined stories: It's *No Way Out* meets *Jagged Edge* with a twist from *The Searchers.*

Some tried to chat for ten minutes before they began the story, to make friends with him. They'd talk about politics or try to teach him a little lesson about art. Some were afraid, their mouths dried out in the middle of the pitch; he could see the tide of fear in their eyes when they could read his boredom. Some talked with Jan like they were long-lost cousins, and then they crumpled in his office. Some were cocky and leaned back into the couch like they owned the room, and they looked up to the ceiling, releasing their stories in a monotone. What was their point? They'd pause before the moment which they were sure would force Griffin to his feet and his desk and a pen, where he would yank his checkbook from a drawer and write them that ticket to a legendary career, to the beginning of their real lives, the promised lives they contained within themselves, inscribed in their genetic code, lives of perfect harmony, where even the bad moments were epic, where tragedy replaced confusion, and ecstasy replaced the merely happy. Yes, Griffin Mill could anoint them, make them Gods, he could grant them everything, he could grant them Christmas in Aspen with Jack Nicholson.

Some worked in teams, like pickpockets or police detectives, completing each other's sentences, playfully contradicting each other, or sometimes flashing murder as one of them botched that fantastic part of this incredible story which would make everyone rich. Some of them even talked about money, about how much the movie would make the first week if Harrison Ford played the hero, how much less if they went with someone else.

They came in with big ideas, rebellion, divorce, revenge, honor. They offered atmosphere: It's sort of a red mood, it's kind of a gritty future, it's funny. Each idea represented a million adjustments to reconcile the difference between the writer's movie of his dreams, which would be the really immortal movie, that tour through the brilliant connections of his freely associating but always focused mind, and the studio's version of that dream, toward the production of which the writer conceded the banal necessity to tell a story. The writers leapt to all this accommodation in anticipation of the thirty-minute audience they'd have with Griffin Mill, that chance of a lifetime to impress their pure, almost unknowable genius on the mediating taste of someone who knew what America wanted to see.

He never said no.

They made their little speeches, then they waited for his response. If he said no, they might challenge him and ask him why, and then they would sell it to him once again, which was futile. He might ask a few questions about the setting, or he would object, moderately, to some unsympathetic quality of the main character, but he would allow them to leave his office thinking that although their chances were slim, yes, yes, yes, there was a possibility. Sometimes, when he walked writers to the door, he pointed to the photographs hanging in the hallway. These were small publicity stills, behind glass, no frame, famous scenes from the movies that had built the studio. He wanted the writers to understand that his door was always open, but they had to bring him a story with crises so powerful that the future could make its images sacred. Kisses while a city burns. Desperate submariners gathered around the periscope. The cavalry leaving the fort. The guilty confronted. The spaceship appearing. Lovers reconciled. Funny men (nervous, innocent) hanging from high places. Monsters. Women screaming. Comedy of inappropriate behavior. Airmen serenading the captain's girl. These were the emblems of the movies' spirit, of love, blood, and speed.

Griffin expected the writers to understand from his silence after a few days that they had failed.

Now he wondered if using time in the service of so much disappointment wasn't a sin.

What happened when writers left him? If the meeting went well for them, did they think that now their lives were different, now their lives had begun? How long before the bogeyman tapped them on the shoulder and said, "No. Not yet. Not you. Not now." What happened to them then, when they were alone and ashamed under the relentless, boring sun of their usual life, burning them with the mundane, with frustration?

If he wasted their time, hadn't he also wasted his own? Somewhere in his mind, wasn't there a fussy little man pushing colored pins into a bulletin board every time a promise was made, and didn't that little man cry for all the pins he'd bought, arranged, and wasted, because the board was covered with pins and he'd never been told what to do with them. He had lost track of the promises.

What about all those meetings? Griffin asked himself. He turned the pages of the calendar. So many meetings. Had he ever said yes? There were some meetings that had led to deals, there were a few deals that had led to movies, but only when writers had come in with producers, or when writers had reputations, when they were on the list, when they'd already sold something or made something. The Writer sending the postcards wasn't on any lists. Griffin guessed he had written a good script, something that attracted the attention of a good agent, and that the agent had then called a few executives, who took his calls and had the Writer meet them. The line in the letter about the agent saying this was a good sign told Griffin that the agent didn't know him very well. He could make a master list of writers and the agents who had sent them to cross-reference the least familiar names, but he would have to ask Jan for help. That was out of the question.

CHAPTER TWO

Griffin told Jan to get Mary Netter. After a moment she told him that Mary was in a meeting. Griffin said it was important, Jan put him on hold, and in a few seconds Mary got on the line.

"What's up? I'm in a meeting."

"I've got a question. How long do you have to wait before you've waited long enough?"

"Is this a plot point?"

"Yes."

"What are we waiting for?"

"This is an etiquette problem, a thank-you letter. How long do you wait for one?"

"Someone sends a gift, she doesn't get a thank-you note and she gets really steamed?"

"He. And he gets mad enough to pick a fight."

"A man is getting this angry? This is a comedy, no?"

"It's just an idea right now."

"If this isn't a comedy, a man shouldn't get that angry. You're describing indignation, which is not for heroes of movies. Whose idea is this?"

"Forget the film for a minute. How long would you wait before you'd waited long enough?"

"When I give a gift to someone and the gift and the person are special to me, I get very excited every time I imagine the person unwrapping the box. If it's for a girl, I think about her saving the ribbon, because I save the ribbon. So, if you've sent the gift by mail, or even if you had the store deliver it, how long does that take? Three days local, a week to New York? If you send something nice and you don't hear back within two weeks, you have a right to be really angry—if they got the gift, of

17

course—unless they got run over by a truck. You imagine your friend with this precious thing and he's enjoying it, but he's not responding. Maybe he hated it. He doesn't know what to say about it. Is that possible?"

"Very possible."

"Well, you think that he hates it, which is just as bad. So you start to resent him, and then you wish you hadn't sent the gift. Maybe it was too extravagant and the person who got it doesn't know what to say, maybe you overestimated the friendship, maybe it's only in your mind. You've sent something valuable, and the person who got it didn't really like you before, and now he's even a little scared of you because only a lunatic would be so generous to a casual acquaintance. Anyway, if the person who sent the gift is really quite proper, then he'd be angry in two weeks. If he brooded a lot, he'd be ready to kill in four or five weeks."

"Who said anything about killing?"

"It's funnier if he wants to kill. This is a comedy, no?"

"You can tell me when you read it, when it's finished."

They said good-bye. Griffin thought that she might have lied about being in a meeting, because she had talked for such a long time without apologizing to anyone in the room. Maybe she had signaled with her hands, like a referee, time out, or maybe she had just talked on while someone in the office sat dumbly, trying to read a memo or a magazine on the coffee table. Maybe she was flattered that he had called her and she didn't want to lose what he was saying, so she ignored, as a matter of survival, that which was not essential, and what was not essential included whomever she had in her office. In that case, if she dropped a meeting for him, then he had not lost too much power at the studio, and Larry Levy would have to fight Griffin's partisans.

Griffin turned the calendar back six weeks. He wished he had asked how long someone might hold a grudge before forgetting about it. A year? Six months? How much hope had he given the Writer? What if the idea the Writer pitched was a comedy and the Writer had made Griffin laugh a few times, or what if the Writer had described a scene that reminded Griffin of his own childhood and he had said so? In either case, the

Writer would have gone home and called his agent and described the meeting as the best of his life, because he had made Griffin Mill laugh or cry. He could have been so rapturous that he'd have called his agent from a pay phone on the lot and then, on his way home, stopped at a car dealer and asked for the price of convertibles. Maybe he took a few friends to dinner that night, that's how confident he was of the impending deal, behaving with the guileless generosity of someone who always has a walletful of twenty-dollar bills.

If the meeting had been early in the week, the Writer might have expected a call from Griffin before the weekend, but his agent would have cautioned him to let a solid week pass, to give Griffin a chance to talk it over with Levison. When had the Writer realized the bad news? Monday afternoon? Had he stayed by the phone at all? Had he checked and rechecked his answering machine? Had he bothered his agent, or his agent's secretary, calling before lunch and then right after lunch to see if Griffin had started the process for making a deal? And then Monday night, and no call. And then Tuesday. More hope on Tuesday. Happiness on Tuesday, confidence on Tuesday. And no call from Griffin on Tuesday. And by the weekend? The agent had told the Writer to face the truth. And did the Writer then fight with his agent? Did the agent tell the Writer he had spoken to Griffin and that Griffin was passing on the project? That was likely. The agent would have known not to call him. Or else he had called, and Griffin hadn't returned that call, and the agent knew to let go, not to make himself a pest. And how long before the Writer wanted to murder?

Griffin was scared. This was not a hypothetical situation. This was not a practical joke. He believed the Writer. He believed that the Writer wanted to kill him. It made sense.

The phone rang. Jan said, "Witcover." A producer. Griffin took the call, and immediately Witcover started to scream at him about the studio's charges for an overseas distribution fee on a picture he had made three years ago.

"That's not my picture," said Griffin. "Who was the exec?"

"Susan Alper, and she's at MGM now, Griffin."

"I'm not in charge of distribution. Why are you calling me?"

"You're supposed to be my friend."

"Then why are you yelling at me?"

"It's how I do business."

"There's something else going on, what is it? You're holding something back from me, I can hear it in your voice."

"Okay. Because you're a fucking executive, Griffin, you're a corporation man, you're not a moviemaker, you're not a showman. I've made five movies. Have you ever read an article in a newspaper and then found a writer and worked on the story together? I mean, all the way from day one to setting it up at a studio, and then finding a director, and then finding a star, and then getting it made, and staying up for postproduction, and then going to a preview in fucking Denver, Colorado, and seen your movie, with your name, on the big screen? Have you, you little shit? A three-line idea from a newspaper, and two years later you take home three million dollars after taxes? A three-line idea and you take it all the way to cable and cassette? Have you ever done that? It's easy to buy things, Griffin. Why don't you come outside and try to sell something?"

"I'm in a meeting right now. Why are you saying all this to me?"

"Because I'm rich, because I don't give a shit. Because you said you liked *Gossip* but you didn't fight for it, and it's in turnaround now, and guess what, I set it up with Susan Alper. So fuck you. That's right. You're history, Griffin." And then Griffin held the phone for no reason, because no one was on the line.

He would need a complete list of everyone he had seen in the last year, would need their phone numbers. Everything was in Jan's desk; she kept phone numbers in the calendar in case meetings had to be canceled. He could ask for it, but he had no excuse. This year's was on her desk. Last year's was probably in a file cabinet. He could send her away, he thought, but if he told her to pick up a story synopsis from the files on another floor, someone might come into the office and find him rummaging around. He would have to wait until night. He often worked until eight or nine. It would be easy to find the calendars.

His own calendar told him that he was having dinner with Bonnie Sherow. He flipped backward through the months; her name appeared at least every other week. She was a production vice-president at Paramount. Griffin had taken her to Mexico, to Cabo San Lucas, for three days, soon after they met, and they talked about moving in with each other. When they decided not to, admitting defeat to convenience, Griffin saw for a moment, in the light of that resignation, that they had been in love. By then it was too late. For a while he thought she was in love with someone new, or testing a possibility, but if she had been, it was over. It had just been a feeling. She never mentioned anyone. He thought she might have been seeing someone who was married, someone at work.

He called her. "I have to cancel tonight."

"I'm sorry."

"I'm the one who's supposed to apologize. Anyway, we've got the Motion Picture Home thing coming up, we'll be together then." Griffin offered this without conviction. They'd made the date months ago. Did she care anymore?

"I'm in a meeting now. Call me tomorrow."

Griffin wanted to rush down the hall and look for a meeting so he could tell everyone in the room about the frightful postcards. Would they comfort him or laugh? The impulse to share his terror brought on a rush of humiliation; he would have felt like the child who calls the teacher "Mommy."

He told Jan to get Larry Levy, who took the call immediately.

"Congratulations," said Griffin, "I just heard the good news."

"I'm looking forward to this, I really am. We're going to have fun, we're going to make some good movies, and we're going to make some money."

"We should have lunch."

"Tomorrow. I'll cancel mine if you'll cancel yours." It was understood that they both had scheduled lunches.

"Done," said Griffin. "Clint Eastwood I can always see."

Griffin's little joke had cost him the first round. They both knew he wouldn't cancel Clint Eastwood. They both knew he wouldn't have lunch with Eastwood unless Levison were there.

Jan buzzed him, this time Sandra Kinroy, an agent, wanted to set up a meeting with a new client. "Has he had anything produced?" asked Griffin.

Kinroy sighed. "Read the script, Griffin."

"Would I want to make this movie?"

"I'd like to see it."

"Then I know I wouldn't want to make it."

"I hear Larry Levy is coming over."

"And you're wondering if you should even bother setting up meetings with me, is that it?"

"Will you read the script? It's a lovely script, he's a lovely man, and you'd do me the favor of a lifetime if you'd read the script yourself. Don't wait for the coverage."

"So there's coverage at other studios and they don't like it."

"Just give this one a chance, Griffin, for me."

She was nothing to him, she had no claim on his obligations, he could have said so, but what was the advantage of a fight with her over nothing? "Send it over." She thanked him. Of course, she knew that he would have it covered first. Each studio sent all submitted scripts to readers, who broke the stories down, described them briefly, and either recommended them or trashed them. Mostly they trashed them. Griffin had started as a script reader. If the script scored well, Griffin would take it home for the weekend and start it. Maybe he would finish it.

When he put the phone down, Griffin contemplated the end to his panic. He closed his eyes and concentrated once again on the postcard Writer. He wanted to talk out loud but worried that someone might hear him. He said, silently, I'm going to choose a writer at random and get back to him and apologize. If that writer accepts my apology, then so should you. And more than that, I will read the script Sandra sends me, I will meet the writer, and if he has any good ideas, I will consider them seriously, and no matter what, I will get back to him.

Now he had a plan. For the next hour and a half he read budget reports and story synopses. Doing his job, he was happy. When Jan said goodbye for the day, he waited until he knew she was gone too long to return for anything she might have left, although nothing near her desk looked like she would want it overnight. Then he closed the door to the hall.

Last year's calendar was in her desk. He took it back to his office and set it next to this year's. So many meetings, so many names, Griffin envied this person who was so busy. Some names were repeated three or four times, and then they disappeared; others were there every day for a week, others only once, some once a week for a year. Producers. Directors. Griffin started to make a list of the one-timers, because they were the writers who had pitched and lost. He closed the book. He didn't want to call someone he hadn't seen in ten months. It would be transparently bizarre.

Should he choose a name at random? Type all the names on individual cards and pull one from the pile? He turned to September, when the temperature had stayed over a hundred for two weeks and the Writer might have interpreted the comfort he felt in Griffin's office as a sign that he and the executive got along well, instead of recognizing the air conditioner as the source of this good feeling. One moment sweating in the parking lot, and a few minutes later cool in Griffin's office, wondering why he had worried so much. On the twenty-first Griffin had seen two writers, Andrea Chalfin at ten in the morning and David Kahane at three-thirty. Andrea Chalfin was directing a movie in Colorado now. She was too busy to send postcards.

This is perfect, thought Griffin. I don't remember Kahane's name, face, or idea. He dialed Kahane's number. This was going to be easy. A woman answered.

"Is David there?"

"No."

"Oh." Griffin didn't know what else to say. "This is Griffin Mill."

"Now it's my turn to say 'oh.'" She knew who he was.

"I promised David I'd get back to him."

"I didn't know he'd seen you."

"Well, it's been a while."

"Do you always work until seven-thirty?"

"Sometimes until ten. How late does David work?"

"I don't think I should give away trade secrets. He'd kill me if I told you that."

"Is he the violent type?"

"Like all writers, he gets drunk before dinner and throws his empty vodka bottles at my head."

"Who are you?"

"June Mercator."

"And what do you do?"

"Baby-sit writers. No. I'm not in the biz at all. I'm an art director for Wells Fargo."

"That's show biz of a sort."

"Paste-ups of interest-rate brochures is show business?"

"You have to make the public happy."

"I have to catch their attention. And most of what I do is seen by people who are already customers. I don't do advertising."

"So David went to the movies tonight?"

"This is Los Angeles. If you don't like rock and roll, what else is there to do?"

"Do you go to the movies much?"

"I used to go with David all the time. I stopped."

"Why?"

"They all end the same way. There's either a chase, a contest, or revenge."

"What if there's love?"

"Someone gets hurt."

"What about comedies?"

"Only if they're really stupid."

"What movie did David go to see tonight?"

"The Bicycle Thief."

"Why didn't you go?"

"I've seen it."

"Is it good?"

"You've never seen it? Shame on you."

He didn't say anything immediately, and in the silence which followed he imagined her waiting for him to say a lot more, why he called, what he wanted, more questions about her, forgetting David. They were on the line silently for too long, and they both hung up.

Griffin found the movie page from that day's paper and looked for *The Bicycle Thief.* It was playing at only one theater, the Rialto in Pasadena.

What if Kahane wasn't there, what if he knew the movie well enough to lie about it to June and use the film as an alibi while he was in bed with someone else? Was June suspicious? Griffin thought he had detected a twang of incredulity in her voice after he had said his name. The effect of his fame never failed to impress him.

It was after seven, the movie had started. It wouldn't take long to drive to Pasadena.

No one knew where he was going. No one was following him. He realized he didn't even have to find David Kahane. He could go wherever he wanted. Choosing to find David, he felt close to the postcard Writer. And so far he couldn't say that Kahane was not the postcard Writer.

On the Pasadena Freeway, Griffin rehearsed his meeting with David Kahane. He would offer his hand, they'd trade comments on the film, and then Griffin would say, "By the way, I'm really sorry I didn't get back to you. It was a good idea, but I'm afraid that Levison is a little more conservative than he should be. Have you had any luck with it at another studio?" He would ask if David wanted to bring in any other ideas or show him a script he might be working on. He could invite David and June to a party, an afternoon barbecue where they could meet other executives and producers. If David was his guest, he knew, everyone at the party would assume he deserved to be there on the strength of something impressive he'd written, since he hadn't had anything produced. He would be invited to meetings. He even might be offered an assignment, sent a script that needed a rewrite, or receive an advance copy of a book, hand-delivered, for his comments. This would save him the struggle of pumping something from his imagination, depleted by too many bewildering meetings.

Griffin hoped David Kahane was smart about money, because he was going to start making lots of it. Griffin would tell his world, "This guy's okay." He worried about how to start his conversation with Kahane. He would ask him if he lived in Pasadena; the question was so wrong, it would make Griffin seem harmless and innocent. He knew where David lived, he had a Hollywood phone number.

He parked on the street a block past the theater. The movie would be over in twenty minutes; he could stand in front of the theater and catch David Kahane on his way out, saving himself a few dollars. He felt the Writer looking over his shoulder, or over his conscience's shoulder, making a clucking noise, as if to say, "Don't cheat. You owe me whatever it costs."

As he paid for the ticket, he wanted to tell the man in the booth that this was the first time he had spent money to see a movie in a few years, probably two years, since he had been stranded in Denver waiting for a plane and he'd had an afternoon to kill. This urge to tell such a pointless anecdote to a stranger embarrassed him so much that he went straight into the theater, skipping the refreshment stand, even though he wanted popcorn. He was hungry. He took a seat in the middle of the back row, between the two doors. He hoped this wasn't one of those theaters where the lights don't go up when the movie is over, because David Kahane, if he was sitting toward the front, could just as easily leave through one of the exits near the screen, and then Griffin might miss him.

CHAPTER THREE

Rome. The 1950s. Griffin watched a father and son on a search for the lost bicycle. Knowing the title, it was obvious that someone had stolen the bike, that this poor man needed it, and that he and his son were now, since the movie was almost over, close to finding the bike and the person who had stolen it. It's a good title, thought Griffin. He liked a movie where the story and the title were the same thing. The father was accusing a man of the theft. Griffin assumed that the father had tracked the man down, that this really was the thief. Here was the danger, though: Everyone in the neighborhood rallied to the thief's defense. They were poor people, perhaps it was a neighborhood of thieves. But, of course, this had to be the thief, it was just too late in the film for a mistaken identity. You'd only do that in the second act, follow a wrong lead. The neighbors, the thief, and even the thief's mother forced the father to back down, after his son ran for a policeman. The policeman arrived but wouldn't arrest the thief. There was no evidence. The father goes with the thief's mother to search the apartment. The point of the scene is to show that everyone is poor, that everyone has a story of misery. The father and son wander around, lost, come to a stadium. There's some kind of game inside—soccer, probably. There are thousands of bicycles parked outside, and then the father sees one bike, alone, on a quiet street. He gives his son bus money and tells him to go away, then he steals the bike. The son does not go away. He sees his father steal the bike. The father is slow, and he's chased and caught. The father and son are let go by the bike's owner, who doesn't want to press charges, because he can see from the situation that the father was desperate. The father and son continue walking and crying.

Griffin was shocked when THE END flashed on the screen. They didn't get the bike. They would never get the bike. The ending was sad. It was so unnecessarily sad, too, because the father had suffered enough; having seen the bicycle thief's apartment, he had reached the point where he could forgive, and instead, he was being forgiven. The father was the Bicycle Thief. Was there a sequel?

The lights came up. Griffin worried how he was going to recognize someone who had bored him for twenty minutes five months before. It was too late to pray for a sign. He watched both rows. A woman passed him and looked at him as though she knew him, or knew who he was. She looked vaguely familiar to him, too, then he remembered. She had introduced him to a production class at the American Film Institute. She caught up with another woman, and he saw her lean into her friend and say something. She tipped her head back toward Griffin. They disappeared into the lobby. The friend returned and walked halfway down the aisle, then looked up toward the projection booth, making a show of searching the room for someone, when all she wanted was a look at Griffin. She got it and walked back out. Behind her was David Kahane.

Griffin supposed Kahane was scowling so hard because he was mad at Hollywood. Griffin stayed in his seat and looked across the aisle, as though he were studying the old plasterwork of the theater. Kahane was about thirty, with the sort of sharp, angular face and straight, thick hair Griffin associated with graduate students. Maybe it was just the wire-framed glasses and the plaid shirt. Griffin was ready to look surprised and happy when Kahane saw him. The writer crossed Griffin's line of sight and went into the lobby. Griffin had prepared his face to say "Hello" or "Hey, how are you?" and there was no one to receive this expression, which soured and withdrew from the missed connection. He considered forgetting the whole idea. Besides, he wanted something to eat.

In the lobby, Kahane walked into the men's room. Griffin knew it would be ridiculous to meet him there. No one shakes hands in the men's room. Griffin leaned against the wall opposite the door and waited.

Kahane came out, drying his fingertips on his jeans. He saw Griffin poised to say hello and he ignored him. He continued out to the street. Griffin followed and called to him on the sidewalk.

"David? David Kahane?" He tried to sound as tentative as possible. Kahane turned. Griffin put his hand out and introduced himself.

"What's the matter," said Kahane, "couldn't you get a screening of it?" It was obnoxious, but he said it with a smile.

"I was feeling restless. I just wanted to sit in a regular movie theater. Same as you."

"You're not thinking of doing an American remake of *The Bicycle Thief*, are you?"

"You want to write it?"

"You'd give it a happy ending."

"Listen, I don't think I ever got back to you on your idea. I'm sorry." Griffin tried to be as casual about this as he could.

"I sort of got the message during the meeting. I dropped the idea, by the way. You were right. It would have made a good script, maybe even a good film with the right director, but it wouldn't have made any money."

Griffin looked for a sign that Kahane was the postcard Writer. He felt that he would know the postcard Writer if he met him. Would the postcard Writer contain himself as well as Kahane? If Kahane was the postcard Writer, wouldn't he be trembling? Griffin asked his routine question, which came as automatically as "How are you?"

"What are you working on these days?"

"A few things."

"I guess you're going home now?"

"Well, what do you have in mind, Mr. Mill?"

"Dinner?"

"I've eaten."

"Let's let the studio buy us a beer?"

"How generous of them."

Griffin saw that Kahane didn't care about him, didn't care that he remembered his broken promise, didn't care that Griffin was offering a bit of friendship. He was not behaving according to the plan. Griffin wanted this man to change his mind about him, to like him and trust him, but he knew that he was tripping over his insincerity. It must have been obvious to Kahane that the embarrassed studio executive was hiding an agenda. They walked down the street, looking for a bar. Kahane pointed to a Japanese bar, Club Hama.

"We'll go there," said Kahane.

They crossed the street. The bar was crowded, at least fifty men, mostly Japanese, in suits. A Japanese woman sat at a piano bar surrounded by men. While she played, a man sitting a few seats away sang into a microphone on a cord. Stiff hostesses in slit dresses delivered drinks and chatted with the customers. Kahane looked relieved.

"It's exactly like this in Tokyo," he said. The hostess came to them, and Kahane spoke to her in Japanese. Griffin felt an inferior sense of adventure. He hated it that this Writer had played a trick on him. He was showing off. They were seated at a booth. The waitress took their order. Kahane had a long chat with her in Japanese. When she left, Kahane told Griffin that she was from Kyoto and wanted to go home.

"Have you been to Japan?" asked Kahane.

"No, actually." Why actually?

"I lived there for a year. I was a foreign exchange student when I was in high school."

"It must have been fun."

"It was. I think about it all the time."

"Have you written about it?"

"No, I told you. You were right, I decided it would have made a good script, but who would care?" No wonder Kahane hated Griffin. The hatred was deserved. He had pitched a story that came from his life, and Griffin had dismissed it. Griffin wanted to defend himself, if the story was so good, Kahane should have written it, anyway.

When the waitress brought the drinks, Griffin reached for his wallet for cash instead of a credit card, so Kahane wouldn't think he was generous only with the studio's money, but she wasn't asking for money yet. He fumbled with his wallet and hoped that Kahane hadn't noticed the awkward gesture. Kahane drank his beer and watched the room. Griffin couldn't tell if Kahane also knew that Griffin had forgotten the story. Was he thinking, Why did I let this stranger tell me my life's best moment wasn't worth writing about? Kahane turned to him.

"You called my home at seven o'clock. You couldn't have seen the whole movie. You came to the theater looking for me. I called home when I got to the theater. I thought I'd lost my briefcase, but it was in the car. I wanted to let my girlfriend know, so she'd stop looking for it. Why did you call? What are you doing here?"

"I'm apologizing."

"For what? All your shitty movies?"

"I said I'd get back to you."

"If I believed everyone in Hollywood who says that, I'd be crazy."

He walked to the piano bar and said something to the pianist. She handed him the microphone. The men at the bar applauded, and he spoke to them in Japanese. They all shook hands, and then Kahane nodded to the happy pianist, who thought this was so wonderful. She started playing the theme song from *Goldfinger*. Kahane sang it in Japanese. Everyone in the club stopped drinking and talking and turned to watch. A few times he must have pronounced difficult words, because a few people clapped or laughed. Griffin wondered if Kahane was making fun of him, if he was really singing about him. Was everyone in the room being told to not stare at him, while the song continued to slander him? Kahane finished singing. The room exploded with applause, cheers, whistles. As Kahane bowed, arms were drawing him to tables, begging him to come and sit for a drink. He put five dollars in the large snifter by the pianist, who wanted to refuse, but he made her keep it. He bowed in Griffin's direction, without eye contact, and walked out. It took a minute for the room to forget him. One of the men at the piano took the microphone and started singing *From Russia With Love*, but everyone in the room groaned and he stopped. The pianist closed the keyboard and walked away. Someone turned on a tape, and now there was different music in the air.

Griffin imagined Kahane telling June Mercator about the evening. He might even tell a few of his friends. How far would the news of this aberration travel? He felt terribly sad, as though nothing in his life had ever gone right, as if he had never once won a prize. He had to remind himself of the prizes he did win.

Griffin studied the cartoon on his cocktail napkin. A woman with big breasts in bed with a bald-headed little man. He had disappointed her somehow. The napkin was wet. Griffin separated the disastrously matched couple, the soaked paper tearing without resistance. Could it even be called paper anymore? Had it reverted to pulp?

He left the money on the table and walked quickly to the door. Outside, he calculated the damage that waited to smear his reputation once this Writer told on him. Best to deny. Deny it all, even the conversation with June Mercator. Would the phone log at the studio show his call? Why would anyone even bother to go so far? Relax, he told himself, there's paranoia and there's silliness. Who did Kahane know?

As he crossed to the shopping plaza where his car was parked, he saw Kahane in a Burger King across the street from the theater. Griffin turned away from his car, to give Kahane another chance. He felt a bit like a counselor at camp, seeking out the homesick kid, the one who won't make his bunk up in the morning, the one whose tears mystify the other children but whose unhappiness is accepted by the staff. Griffin didn't know what he was going to say, but it didn't matter now. The situation was in his hands. Besides, Kahane was a bit drunk. From outside the Burger King, Griffin could see Kahane dipping French fries into a puddle of ketchup. He was drinking coffee. The snack of a college student, thought Griffin.

Kahane looked up and saw him. He lurched away from the table and walked out the other door. Griffin followed. Kahane crossed the street to the theater and entered a narrow passage in the direction of a sign that pointed to ALWAYS FREE PARKING IN THE REAR. Griffin had to run hard to keep up. He called after Kahane, "David, stop!"

Kahane turned and waited for Griffin to catch up.

"What do you want?"

"You sing very well."

"Great, the studio has a record label, let's put out an album."

"Why are you so mad at me?"

"I'm not mad at you. I'm just an asshole, okay? It's just my nature. It's the way I am."

"I guess I must look pretty silly to you. I mean, driving out here to deliver a message you already got."

"It makes you almost human."

"Why are you so hostile to me?"

"If I am, I'm sorry."

"Have you ever sent me a postcard?" He had to ask. He had to know.

"What kind of postcard?" Kahane, who had been fiddling with his keys, using the noise as a sign of his impatience, put them back into his pocket. He was curious.

"You don't like me, do you?"

"I have no strong feelings about you, one way or the other."

"The truth, David."

"I told you the truth. I don't really care about you. I don't spend a lot of time thinking about you."

"But you're mad at me for not getting back to you, aren't you?"

"I told you, I don't expect anything different."

"So you do have a low opinion of me."

"You want me to say I hate you?"

"Of course not."

"I think you do. And I didn't come here tonight to make you happy." Kahane took the keys out of his pocket and shook them once, this time to announce that the audience was over. He started to walk away.

"One more thing," said Griffin, who stayed in the alley as Kahane squeezed between two cars in the parking lot. Kahane kept walking. Griffin followed him. It was harder for Griffin to move between the cars, and he was aware that Kahane was slim. Griffin tried to convince himself that Kahane was, after all, the postcard Writer. This would explain the bad behavior. Griffin had made a perfect guess, as brilliant in its own way as the selection of a screenplay for a production that goes on to earn a hundred and fifty million dollars. A psychic beam had locked him into his secret tormentor. Kahane was the postcard Writer, and his reactions to Griffin—the mean answers to friendly questions, the humiliating display of talent, the indifference—were all dramatizations of Griffin's behavior toward him. Griffin wanted to tell Kahane that they were even now, there was no need to play this game of bully boy.

Kahane stopped at a new black Saab; the dealer's sticker was still glued inside the window. Griffin wondered where an unknown writer earned the money for such a car. He expected an old Datsun, a first car, not a reward. Maybe it was June Mercator's car. Griffin caught up with him.

"New car," said Griffin.

"Surprised? You wonder where I get the money?"

"I guess you'll tell everyone."

"Tell them what? What's going on, Griffin? You didn't come here to say something about my story, you forgot it as soon as I was out the door. What is going on?"

Griffin didn't answer. He couldn't speak. He dragged his foot along the ground, sideways, and then he knelt down, beside the rear tire. He toyed with the plastic cap to the air valve and began, slowly, to unscrew it. When it came off in his hand, he pressed the tiny pin with the edge of his thumbnail, and he thought about telling Kahane the truth.

"What are you doing?" said Kahane.

How would Kahane take the answer, that he had come to appease someone who was sending him angry postcards, and that he had felt that the simple act of offerring a second chance to one person he had ignored might, in some cosmic way, get back to that offended man, that Writer of awful hate mail. As the air hissed out of the tire, smelling of gas stations and rubber, Griffin looked up at Kahane, who looked down with the confused expression of someone trying to understand something being screamed at him in a language he didn't understand. Kahane bent down to look Griffin in the face. Griffin wanted to smile, to let Kahane see the irony of the moment, now that they were equal.

"Griffin, what's going on?"

"I'm sorry," said Griffin. "I wish I could explain." Griffin pushed Kahane down from his unsteady balance on the balls of his feet. Kahane reached out to grab something on the car, but the door handles were recessed and there was nothing to hold. With his arms out, he fell over, and Griffin stood up and then dropped on his knees to Kahane's chest, like a TV wrestler, and Kahane grunted and swore. Griffin felt the strength of that legendary mother who pulled the car off her child; the power of the universe was in his hands. He sat on Kahane's chest and held his throat in those hands, and he saw what it was to choke a man to death.

Kahane tried to throw Griffin off with a few thrusts of his legs, but Griffin had never felt such focus before. Nothing could move him. Kahane was gagging, throwing spit on Griffin's pants, but it was too late for him to yell. The surprise of the attack had taken his breath away. He died with his eyes closed.

Griffin took Kahane's wallet and watch. He considered putting the body in the car and driving it away from the lot, but then he would have to take a taxi back to his own car. He would just leave him and walk away. He rolled the body under the car. No one would see it at night. He put the cap back on the valve; the action of threading it was a comfort, he was sorry when he let it go. He crawled away, hiding below window level of three cars before standing up. He went the long way around the parking lot to the street.

When he got to the main boulevard, he looked behind him. Nothing. No one. As he drove past the theater on the way to the freeway, the audience was leaving the final show.

All right, he said to himself, suppose you're in court and they're asking you how you felt, what would you say? Honestly? Detached, maybe. There was a sensation of terrific exhaustion, but that was from the physical strain of wrestling. It was not impossible to kill.

He pulled off the freeway in Hollywood and dropped the wallet and watch in a gas station dumpster. At the next red light, on Sunset

Boulevard, his right foot started to shake on the brake pedal. He asked himself if this was fear or guilt, and he couldn't answer. He took Sunset to Beverly Glen and drove into the canyon.

His house was quiet and fresh, pleasantly unfamiliar, the way it was when he came home from long trips. Night-blooming jasmine cast its scent into his bedroom.

After a shower he took a bottle of tranquilizers from his medicine cabinet. He tapped two pills into his hand but thought, no, and threw the two pills into the toilet. He dropped the rest of the pills in the water and flushed them away. It had been two years since he had taken any, his system was clean, he didn't really drink more than a few beers or glasses of wine a week, no drugs anymore, this was no time to start. As he watched them drown, he knew he had made the right decision, even the brave decision. He didn't think of it as a protective maneuver, against a sudden urge to kill himself, but instead it was a renunciation, an exercise in discipline. Sedation inhibits dreaming. If he was going to suffer nightmares, better to let them come as they wanted, as they needed, and not try to scare them away with little pills; all the small, bad dreams would collect in an ugly hive, waiting for him, and he couldn't keep them away forever, not even with addiction. What else would he suffer? He expected the name David to bother him. He hoped it wouldn't show up in scripts. Yes, and for a while he would be nervous every time he saw a cop, but this, too, would pass.

He slipped into bed and felt high excitement. He was tempted to get up and drink a glass of chamomile tea, but the thought of all that effort— get up, turn on lights, walk downstairs, step on the cold tile, open up cabinet, open up box of tea, remove tea bag, turn on flame, lean against counter, wait for water to boil, wait for tea to steep, look at clock, come back upstairs—was overwhelming. He lowered himself into his exhaustion, which welcomed him. He looked through the darkness to the Writer and searched his heart for all the sincerity he could squeeze from it and tried to adjust for the interference of pride. He said aloud, "I hope you understand what I've done." Then he fell asleep.

In the morning he found a postcard attached to his newspaper. It was the kind of all-occasion card that little gift shops sell, an airbrush collage of a slice of cherry pie, a 1957 Buick, red lips, fried eggs, bacon, and a half of a kiwifruit. All of these images floated over a Rocky Mountain backdrop, a forest receding to a snowcapped range. He turned it over. The writing was dense, almost impenetrable.

> *Griffin—*
> *You said you'd get back to me.*

Griffin looked at the card: IMAGES WITH AN APPETIZING DIFFERENCE. How many stores in Los Angeles sold this card? The card reminded him of a Betty Boop cartoon in which Earth is for sale and is auctioned off to the planets. The lowest bidder, Saturn, wins. Somehow Earth's magnetic core, a horseshoe magnet on a string, is removed and put in Saturn's pocket. Gravity is reversed. Everything floats from the land. Finally the magnet is returned and order is restored.

Now he had killed a man, and what good had it done him? He looked through the newspaper. The body would have been found too late for the morning edition. There was nothing about it yet. The death would probably catch some attention, but was it brutal or ugly enough to be really newsworthy? What would the police think? A simple mugging. No one would know it was a sacrifice.

How long would it take this gesture of appeasement carried on the scent of that bloodless death to reach the Writer? Stuffing a body under a car in Pasadena to convince someone to leave you alone is a complicated message. The Writer was having fun with Griffin, so why should he stop and kill him?

Griffin drove to the studio, hoping he had addressed this message correctly. He had sent something by slow mail, but he was certain it would arrive. He was positive.

CHAPTER FOUR

"**N**obody leaves my office until we agree on fifteen reasons for why we go to the movies." Levison looked around the room. "Alison, when was the last time you bought a ticket to see a movie?"

Alison Kelly, his story editor, covered her face with her hands. "I am so embarrassed," she said. "But I just hate to stand in lines. I think it's been two months. What can I say, I go to screenings."

Levison stood up. "From now on, everyone in this room has to go to a movie theater and pay to see a movie, sneak previews don't count, at least once a month." He turned to Griffin. "Griffin, when was the last time you bought a ticket to see a movie?"

"*The Bicycle Thief,* last night." As soon as he said it, he realized what he had done. He had confessed.

"Okay," said Levison, "why did you go?"

"Because it's a classic and I've never seen it."

"And why didn't you have it screened?"

"I wanted to feel the audience reaction."

"What was the reaction?"

"They loved it."

"Who were they?"

"People who hate the movies we make." Better to go on the attack. Maybe not.

"Did you like it?"

"It's great. Of course."

"No remake potential?"

"We'd have to give it a happy ending."

"What if we set it in space, another planet. *The Rocket Thief?*" He was grinning. This was a joke.

"A poor planet?"

"There you go," said Levison. "Right away we're talking about something we've never seen in a science-fiction film, and that's a poor planet. How come space is always rich?"

"Luke Skywalker's farm in *Star Wars* was pretty run-down."

"Fine," said Levison. "And it worked, and what I'm saying is, that's why we have these meetings, to come up with images, to come up with characters and story ideas, so we're not at the mercy of whoever comes through the door. So we can contribute, so our own ideas can get made. Now. Let's start at the beginning. Why do we go to the movies? Give me some reasons."

Hands were raised. Levison ran to the always ready easel with its large tablet of clean poster paper and, with a marking pen, quickly scribbled one through fifteen.

"One," he said. "Griffin went to see a classic. This list should not be in any special order of priority. You'll notice I don't want to start with the clichés, like escape or entertainment. So we'll say—and this is a legitimate reason to go to the movies—we'll say, 'We go to see classics.'"
He wrote CLASSICS on the paper. Then he wrote next to two, ENTERTAINMENT, and next to three, ESCAPE.

"Mysteries," someone said. MYSTERIES was added.

"Doesn't anyone go to the movies for sex?" asked Levison. "Don't guys choose movies that they hope will turn on their girlfriends?" Levison grinned and wrote SEXUAL PROVOCATION.

"New fashions?"
STYLE.

"I like driving fast after a James Bond film."
ENERGY.

"What about movie stars?"
STARS.

"I'm always happy looking at Paris."
TRAVEL.

"Comedy."
LAUGHS.

"Horror films."

SCREAMS.

"Songs."

SONGS.

"Love stories."

LOVE STORIES.

"Are we talking about types of movies or reasons that we go?" Drew asked.

"Whatever gets you to the theater," said Levison.

"I like the crowd," said Drew. "I like other people."

COMMUNITY.

Griffin pressed back into the green couch. He thought about excuses. First he would have to say something to the people in the room. Once the body was discovered, and it was already in a morgue, he knew that someone would say, "This writer was killed outside that theater you went to last night, Griffin, did you know that?" And he would answer, "That's the last time I go out in public." Some kind of light remark to get away from the specific murder into the territory of a world gone mad.

"Sometimes," said Drew Posner, "I have to admit I go to the movies not so much for escape—well, I guess it's a kind of escape, but it's more—it's for comfort. It's sort of everything, it doesn't matter what kind of film, just as long as it's a movie."

COMFORT.

"I know they're not popular now," said Mary, "but I've always liked big costume epics."

PERIOD.

"Fair enough," said Levison. "The point of this exercise is to think about what we like, not what we think we should like, or what we think the public will like or what we think the public already likes. And that's fifteen. Let's get sixteen. Who's going for it?"

Griffin raised his hand. "Usually I go to the movies to see what everyone else is seeing, so I can talk about it, so I don't feel left out. When I was in the fourth grade, all the cool kids in my class had seen *The Great Escape*. I hadn't. But I acted like I had."

Levison held the chalk to the board, trying to find the one word.
"Try lemmings," said Drew.
PEER PRESSURE.
"Now that we know why we go to the movies, the next step will be to look for projects that engage us on these basic levels. Class dismissed."
Griffin wanted the day to stop until the afternoon edition of the *Herald* came out. He returned to his office and closed the door. He called the studio store and asked if the afternoon papers were in. They were.
Jan looked up from her script as he left. He marched to the store, picked up the paper, dropped his quarter, and marched back to his office. He was gone for five minutes. He passed Jan and closed the door. He put the paper on the desk. He felt the same anticipation for the news as he did when the first reviews of one of the company's films came out. It was on the ninth page.

MAN FOUND DEAD IN THEATER PARKING LOT

A theater projectionist leaving his job after midnight discovered the body of David Kahane, 29, in the parking lot of the Rialto Theater in Pasadena. A spokesman for the Pasadena Police said that Kahane had been dead at least two hours before the body was discovered. The cause of death has not been identified. Kahane, a part-time writer, was a resident of Hollywood.

Would the Writer read this and get the message? Griffin wasn't sure. Why did they call him a part-time writer? Griffin felt sorry for Kahane. Probably the reporter had a screenplay in his desk, or ideas for a script, and a friend or two in the entertainment department of the paper, so he had a mean sense of the fringes of the business. Poor June Mercator, who probably loved Kahane, would she stay with him if she hadn't loved his writing? That was too hard a question. Blinded by love, she might have thought he was Melville. Would she spend the next few days reading Kahane's unpublished stories and unproduced scripts? Here was a sentence Griffin wished he could say: I have killed exactly the right man.

Griffin looked at his messages. A call from an agent. A call from the Marketing department. A call from Business Affairs. A call from a writer. A call from an agent. A call from an agent. A call from Levison. A call from his lawyer. A call from London. Had Kahane ever been this busy? Was the Writer ever this busy?

Jan called him on the intercom. Walter Stuckel was in the outer office. Griffin told Jan to tell him to wait a minute. He got off the phone. He counted to ten, then to twenty, then to twenty-seven. He went to the door, better to meet Stuckel more than halfway.

"Hello, Walter." Stuckel was on his feet, reading memos faced away from him on Jan's desk. When Griffin extended his hand, Stuckel looked up slowly, and this refusal to play along, which in anyone else would have provoked annoyance, scared Griffin.

Stuckel took his hand. He was about fifty-five, with thick white hair brushed forcefully away from a severe part; anyone in a corporation would recognize that he was not an administrative executive. He wore a turquoise blazer and black pants and brown Florsheim loafers. He had mottled pink-and-white skin. He squinted, just a little, not to avoid the sun but to focus his examination. "We should talk," he said.

Griffin brought him into his office. Instead of taking a seat by the couch, he sat behind his desk, forcing Stuckel to take a hard-backed chair. He offered coffee. Stuckel refused it, politely.

"Okay, Walter," said Griffin, "don't tell me you've come to pitch a story."

"I've got a few."

"I bet you do, Walter."

"But I'm not a writer."

"If the stories are good, we can always hire someone to make them work." Griffin didn't like the subject. His heart was pounding.

"Did you ever have a meeting with David Kahane?"

"Yes. Quite a while ago."

"Did you know he's dead?"

"Good Lord, he was younger than me, what happened?"

"Why don't you tell me?"

Griffin wanted to stop time. "Walter, tell me everything you're thinking about, right now."

"Did you know I used to be a cop?"

"FBI, right?"

"That too. I got a call from Pasadena homicide today. David Kahane was murdered last night."

"No."

"And you called his house around seven o'clock. His girlfriend told you he was going to see a movie in Pasadena."

"I don't even remember the name of the movie."

"*The Bicycle Thief.* You went."

"No, I didn't."

"You went. You met Kahane at the theater, you got drunk with him in a Japanese restaurant, and he left before you did. Then he went to a McDonald's. That was the last time anyone saw him alive. Griffin, why do you deny it?"

"What do the police think happened?" It was a Burger King, not a McDonald's. Already the story was getting lost. This cheered Griffin and gave him hope.

"They think he was murdered for his wallet and his watch. It happens every day. I can tell the police you're acting like you've got something to hide, and they'll haul you into the station for questioning. Or I can let you speak to them over the phone. Or they can come here. Or they can drop this altogether. I don't think they'll do that."

"Of course, I'd want to cooperate any way I can."

"There was a party in Malibu a few years back, music people. A lot of drugs. A lot of rum."

Griffin supposed this was Stuckel's way of saying that this story was about black people.

"And there was a security guard, to keep gate-crashers away. He had a gun. One of the guests wanted to play with it. The guard gave him the gun. A few minutes later the guard was dead. The police were the second call. And the matter was taken care of."

"Who did they call first?"

"I wouldn't tell you if I knew. I have to say, though, that I admire your tactics. Stonewall. Deny everything, it's your word against theirs. As long as nobody saw you actually kill the man, and as long as you have nothing to connect you, except for, well, how many meetings did you have?"

"I only met him once."

"Not counting last night."

"Okay," said Griffin, "you're right. I saw him last night. And I did know he's dead, I saw the paper."

"Then why didn't you say so?"

"Good God, Walter, I don't want to get involved."

"Very good. I'll tell that to the police."

"I'll call them myself. I'll say I met him at the theater, we got drunk together at a Japanese bar, he had to go home, I didn't feel sober enough to drive, he left, that was the end of it. I'll tell them, when they ask, that I went to see him because he'd pitched me an idea, I loved it so much, I wanted to buy it, and I didn't want to wait until he was home to tell him. I was that happy for him, and for me. That's the truth. That's what I'll tell them. I'll go there right now." How could anyone, how could Walter Stuckel, not believe this? It was so simple. And if they didn't believe it, Griffin would stick to this line, because it was easy to tell and easy to remember. It made sense.

"No. We'll have them come here."

"I don't want to inconvenience them."

"You're talking like someone who's guilty. You're not guilty, are you?"

"The usual neurotic guilt."

"That's a joke. This is murder. I was a cop. You're behaving like you killed him. If you act this way with the police, they'll be suspicious."

"How should I act?"

"You tell them everything. They're trying to solve a murder."

"I haven't killed anyone."

"I'll let you know when they're coming."

Stuckel left. Griffin wasn't sure what had happened. Was he under suspicion for murder? Or was there only the routine questioning of everyone who might have information about the last hours of a victim? There was no reason for him to have killed Kahane; rather, there was no discoverable reason for the murder. Griffin considered that this might have been the most private event of his life. He could go on a witness stand and describe the hour he'd spent with Kahane, then describe their parting in the restaurant. Why did they leave separately? Griffin wanted to hear more music. Kahane was feeling sick. Kahane wanted to get back to his girlfriend. No one would doubt him.

Levison called. A director under contract was looking for a romantic comedy. Would Griffin check around for a few scripts? Griffin would. He pushed Kahane and Stuckel from his mind as he dialed the phone himself. He was working.

Griffin was shocked by how little guilt he felt. It almost made him want to see a therapist. This is probably why I'm not married, why I don't have a family, he thought. He couldn't imagine how he could go to someone with this problem. Did the seal of confession apply? What would a therapist say? I can't help you; your remorse is misplaced.

When he took Bonnie Sherow to Cabo San Lucas, she had annoyed him by saying how grown-up it was to take that kind of vacation. "I feel like such a grown-up," she had said when they were alone in the room after the bellboy left.

"What do you mean, 'grown-up'?" he'd snapped. "You think we're just kids and we're playacting. This is real. I don't feel like I haven't earned the right to do what I do." He didn't know then what he was really saying, he was just tired of Bonnie, probably, and looking for a fight. Bonnie knew then, when she covered herself and wouldn't make love to him until later that night, after a lot of tequila, that his little outburst marked the end of it for them. He knew his anger at her was wrong. Bonnie had looked at him with disappointment and sadness. Was he a grown-up now that he had killed a man? Bonnie had meant responsible, contained, independent, capable of decision, capable of spending money. There was also a sense of gravity, the feeling of being centered. He knew twenty-five-year-olds who were given charge of millions of dollars for film budgets. Were they grown-ups? He was thirty-one and sometimes felt exhausted. Was he a grown-up? David Kahane had spent years reaching for a brass ring. What had he learned? Was he a grown-up?

Griffin wondered if he would have to kill again. He supposed a therapist would tell him that he was waiting to be caught, and if he were caught, then yes, he must have been waiting, but what if he weren't caught? Let's suppose I live a long time and die with a smile, thought Griffin, and only I know that I killed. Am I the tree falling silently in the forest because no one hears it? If you get away with murder, is it murder?

And if he went to an analyst, and he trusted the analyst enough to confess the murder, and the analyst asked him why he killed David Kahane, what would he answer? Because I had to. Because he was there. Because I had hit bottom and there was nowhere left to go. Because I've never been to war, and I needed to kill a man.

Why did you need to kill a man?

Because he was there.

What if I take out an ad in *Variety*, he thought, a small ad, anonymous, telling the postcard writer that I want to meet him? What if I don't show up, what if I hide, watch him, see him, and then, later, kill him. No witnesses. An alibi. Go to San Francisco for the weekend and fly down under another name on another airline. Kill him, go back to San Francisco, and come home as Griffin Mill.

Jan was in the room. "Griffin?" She looked at him with doubt. "Are you okay?"

"Why?" How long had this reverie lasted? Had he missed a ringing phone?

"Walter Stuckel, what did he want? Was this about the postcards?"

It was time to take charge. He looked at Jan with an equal blend of impatience, condescension, and affection. "Jan." It was all he had to say. When she left the room and closed the door, he raised a triumphant fist in the air.

He wrote, "I said I'd get back to you" on a piece of notepaper. Then he wrote, "It's time we talked." He paused. Now what? He crossed out that last line about naming the time and place. The line was weak, a kind of appeasement. It was too familiar. "No more cards. It's my move now, but I'm giving it to you. Let's do it soon." He called *Variety* and got a price for a small ad. They preferred a check but accepted cash. Cashier's check? they asked. No, said Griffin, cash.

On his way home that night he stopped at a bank machine and took out two hundred dollars. When he got home, he put the money and the message in an envelope and addressed it to *Variety*. He didn't have any stamps, because he never mailed anything from home. He bought stamps from a post-office machine in the morning.

June Mercator called him at nine-thirty. Jan told him her name with a stupid innuendo, as though it were an old affair he was trying to stop. He wanted to say "Who?" but he took the call without a word.

"Hello, June. My God, I just found out about David. How are you?"

"Oh, I'm not very good, I guess. It hasn't really hit me yet. It's very complicated."

"I can imagine." Why was she calling?

"I'm just watching myself go through the motions of my own life." Griffin sensed that she didn't want to talk about this now, that she wanted to control the call, that she wasn't feeling particularly emotional and wasn't up to faking it.

"This is a blow to all of us," said Griffin. "Have the police . . . have they made any progress?"

"No." Then she didn't say anything.

"You know, I went to the theater after I called you."

"Yes." Griffin wished she had said, "I know." Her "Yes" just hung there, a challenge. He had already talked too much. Of course this is why she's calling. "Yes, I wanted to talk to David about an idea. I had something he would have been good for."

"You were going to give him an assignment?"

"If I say yes, I'll be lying. I was going to talk to him about something, to see if he was interested, to see what ideas he might have."

"What did he say?"

"He said he'd call me in the morning. He didn't have his date book with him, but he'd try to fit me in." Griffin said this with a touch of bemused pity, to let June know he wasn't fooled by David but didn't hold the game against him.

A low sound came from June, a kind of sigh. Griffin heard a little exasperation with this bit of silly diplomacy, as though David were still alive, a little reproach directed at his soul, a little anger at herself for staying with him when it was just this kind of obvious gesture in the direction of pride that had kept her lover so far from success.

"Poor David," she said.

"Did he have parents and stuff, family?"

"Everything. Parents, a brother, a sister, a grandmother. A niece."

"When's the funeral?"

"You don't have to go." There was a new sound in her voice, she was too quick, he thought; she was embarrassed about something.

"When is it?"

"Tomorrow morning."

"I'll be there."

"Griffin, have the police spoken to you?"

"We've had contact."

"Good. I mean, maybe you saw something. Maybe you don't even know it, maybe you saw the killer, maybe you saw a car or something that's been near other murders."

"No. I hate to say this, but I didn't see anything."

"You don't know that."

The call ended. Griffin was surprised by the edge of desperation in June Mercator's voice. When he'd spoken to her the night of the murder, she'd sounded ready to leave Kahane. Now she was crying over small clues. Griffin wondered if Bonnie Sherow would miss him if he died.

The next morning, he didn't wait until the office for *Variety*, he bought it at a liquor store and ripped the back page as he searched for his small ad. "No more cards. It's my move now, but I'm giving it to you. Let's do it soon." He read it over three times, a dozen times, aware of a surge of pride, authorship, which relented only when a kind of stage fright chewed its way through his satisfaction. It was so naked, no phone number, no box number, something to invite a bit of curiosity from the casual reader. He realized Jan might see the ad and show it to him, so he was glad he hadn't ordered NO MORE POSTCARDS. If Jan was to bring it to him, he would tell her to get back to work. This led him to consider firing her. On the one hand, he thought, she's too caught up in the postcards, the next secretary might pass them on to him without comment, but if his plan worked, if the Writer left him alone, whether because he was dead or scared or etherically placated, they would stop. On the other hand, Jan would tell the replacement about the postcards, and if they continued, even for a short time, he would have to tell more lies.

CHAPTER FIVE

Griffin did not want to have lunch with Larry Levy. At eleven he might have been able to cancel, and then Levy would have had to eat alone, or call someone and admit he was suddenly free, and all during that meal Levy would have worried about with whom Griffin's important meeting was, but the crack about Clint Eastwood had cost him the advantage.

He forced himself to believe that he was as much of a threat to Levy as Levy was to him, that Levy knew he was being hired as a wild card, not as a king. The restaurant Levy had chosen, a shiny Italian kitchen on Melrose, was not an obvious choice, like Le Dome or The Grill, one of those student dining halls in the campus of Hollywood. This suggested to Griffin a purpose to the lunch, since eating at one of the usual places would have made a public statement. Everyone would know by now that Levy was going to the studio, and they would have been interrupted. So Levy wanted to talk. It hadn't occurred to Griffin until now that Levy was scared about coming to the studio. Griffin wouldn't plan a strategy for the lunch, something Levy's intimidating energy could upset; no, with faith in Levy's self-doubts he could have fun.

Levy was already at the restaurant when Griffin arrived. The hostess, a thin woman in black, led Griffin to the table in the restaurant's second room. Griffin knew her from a restaurant in Beverly Hills where she had also worked the door; on the way to Levy she told Griffin she shared ownership with the chef of this one. Griffin said, "Congratulations," but recognized a touch of jealousy for the woman. Why? he wondered, and silently answered himself, Because she created this out of nothing.

Levy started from his chair, and Griffin waved him down. He wore a dark blue suit, too heavy for the day, but it had been cool in the morning. He was almost tall and had the packed look of someone with a personal trainer. Griffin, twenty pounds too heavy, was jealous of that, but somewhere along the way Levy had met a clumsy plastic surgeon, and his nose, though reasonably well shaped, was a size too small for his face, and in combination with his heavy, dark eyebrows and thin hair, his look alternated between sinister and silly.

"You know you won't have to wear a suit when you come to the studio. Levison likes sport jackets." A fair beginning.

"I'll keep them in storage until an oil company takes over and asks for a new executive image."

"Is that the latest? Is Mobil buying us out?"

"Who knows? Sometimes I think about going back to business affairs. Production is always doomed after a takeover, but business affairs hang on."

"That's right, you come from business affairs." Griffin said this with mild surprise, with the implication now floating in the current between them that good production people never came from business affairs, or that business affairs might have spawned a few good production people, but they were always tainted. "Well," he said, "you weren't there for very long." This was certainly obnoxious. Griffin took the lead.

"For about an hour," said Levy. "When I was at Warner Brothers, I kept making deals for scripts that I'd never read, and it just got to me after a while, because there were all these writers making seventy grand against three hundred, and I'd never heard of ninety percent of them, they'd never had movies made, and then the scripts would get delivered, and I'd get a notice to release a check, and then I'd get an order to make a deal for a rewrite with a new writer for another ungodly piece of change, and then, when the studio finally did make a movie, it was a script they bought in turnaround from somebody else because Sydney Pollack or Chevy Chase was attached. So after a year of this I started to read the scripts, every script we made a deal on, every rewrite, every draft, and after I'd read three hundred of them, literally three hundred scripts, I told them to bring me into production or I'd quit. And they didn't, so I quit and went to work at United Artists, and they liked me and I liked them and I made friends and I got a good reputation, and I was lucky and three scripts I developed got made into movies and one of them cost nine and did a hundred and thirty-five million, and Levison made me an offer I couldn't refuse. That's my story."

"And now you're here to run the studio."

"I hear that Levison put out feelers to two studios saying he was available for the right price. If he goes . . ." Levy spread his hands. The gesture meant, "I'm ready."

The waiter came and took their orders. Levy asked for a salad, and Griffin, buttering a roll, asked for a small pizza. He was glad he hadn't come to the table with a strategy, because he would have chosen the same tactics, and the same measly lunch as Levy, and now he was calm, while Levy looked forlorn that he was having only a salad and couldn't break down for a roll or pasta. Somewhere Levy had read a book about power lunching, but he must have skipped the lesson on keeping eye contact with the person across the table, and to avoid staring at his carbohydrates. Griffin knew he showed extreme confidence to order more food than Levy. It was a small battle, but he had won it.

"Are you ever tempted to leave?" asked Levy, watching Griffin butter another roll.

"I'm happy where I am."

For the rest of the lunch they talked about movie stars and directors. Levy liked to gossip, and Griffin let him. He finished his salad quickly and refused an offer of a slice of Griffin's small pizza.

When the waiter asked, Griffin even ordered dessert. It was chocolate cake. He offered a taste to Levy.

"No thanks."

"You sure?"

Levy waved his hand, brushing aside his tactics, and accepted. Griffin fed him the cake off his fork.

When Griffin got back to the studio, Jan left her desk and followed him inside his office.

"What's the matter?" he asked.

"You got a phone call from the Pasadena Police, and Walter Stuckel came back, and Celia told me that they called Levison too." Jan had recommended Celia for the job, and she always told her as much as she could.

"Do you think she told everyone else?" Griffin wished he had said something like, "Do you know what this is about?" He tried to cover. "It looks like I was one of the last people to see someone before he got murdered. A writer. Someone who pitched to me once."

"How awful. Did you know him well?"

"No, not at all."

"Don't worry about Celia. And don't be silly, there's no shame in being a witness."

"I wasn't a witness. I didn't see anything."

"I mean, there's no shame in being the last person to see someone alive."

"The problem is that any special attention is bad. I get enough attention. And I told Walter, all I did was see the guy after a movie, that's it. Get me Levison. I'd better speak to him before I call back the police."

Jan picked up the phone on his desk and used the intercom to get Celia. "Hi, is he in? It's Griffin." She waited a beat, then handed the phone to him. Levison wanted to see him immediately.

He left his office and walked down the hall, getting angrier with every step at the Pasadena Police and at Stuckel. He wanted to yell at them, find out why they just didn't call his mother and his homeroom teacher, for God's sake. Celia told him to go right in.

Levison left his desk, shut the door behind Griffin, and indicated the couch. There was a crudely drawn graph on the poster paper, a curve divided by three slashes. Underneath the third was written THE MONSTER DIES TWICE. It was an act breakdown for a story. Levison ripped it down when he saw Griffin's attention drift to the board.

"So what's all this?" said Levison. "Did you know this guy? Did we ever hire him for anything?"

"I was thinking about it."

"I never heard of him."

"Sometimes I like to give a kid his shot."

"Somebody beat you to it."

"Why is everybody in on this?"

"Why didn't you tell us, as soon as you heard he was dead, that you'd seen him?"

"Because all I did was see him. Because I have more important things to do than rock the goddamn boat right now."

"Meaning you need to cover your flanks while Levy is approaching?"

"Meaning this job is hard enough without making a spectacle of myself. If I'd thought about it a little more, I would have realized that there was no avoiding it, and I should have just told you as soon as I heard he was dead."

"I mean, I'm your friend. Forget boss. Friend. When you're in trouble, you're supposed to call me."

"Am I in trouble?"

"Of course not, no. You didn't kill him."

"So what should I do now?"

"Let Walter Stuckel take care of this for you. We want to keep your name out of the papers, and he knows how to handle that kind of thing. After the cops see you, Walter'll give them passes to a screening where they can sit two rows behind Michelle Pfeiffer, and this will all go away."

Griffin liked the turn of the conversation, from exasperation to action. Levison stood up, since the meeting was over.

Leaving him, Griffin felt a kinship with Levison. He wanted to invite Levison and his wife to dinner, he pictured himself washing a head of lettuce and Levison knocking on the door, with a bottle of good wine in his hand. Just the three of them, he wouldn't even have a date, they could all relax. And if they drank too much and didn't want to drive home, he would give the Levisons his guest room. It would be nice to make breakfast for them, or better yet, come downstairs and find them already scrambling the eggs. How much trouble am I really in? he wondered.

Walter Stuckel called to set up a meeting with two detectives from the Pasadena Police, at five.

"Don't talk too much," he said. "They go on these interviews all the time, and they don't usually visit young bucks at movie studios. They might try to trip you up, but if they suspect anything, it's only that you really did see something, and you think you're too much of a big shot to help out. They might also think that this is a gay thing, some kind of gay murder, you know, maybe he came on to some guy, maybe some guy came on to him, and they'll probably throw a couple of questions in along that line. Did you know anything about his private life? And they wouldn't be at all suspicious of you except that you saw him, and you didn't call them as soon as you knew he was murdered."

"How should I answer that?"

"The truth. You are a big shot. You don't have time to get involved in something you can't change. Don't try to be their friend, Griffin, that's my job."

"So what'll you do, meet them at your office and come up here?"

"Right, and I'll take them the good way, through the back lot. See you later." End of call.

Griffin went to the bathroom, washed his face, and looked at himself in the mirror. He practiced a few insincere smiles, then washed his face again, this time with water so hot, it left his hands pink. He thought about Larry Levy, and feeding him the chocolate dessert, and wasn't so scared of the police anymore. He unknotted his tie and put it together close to the throat. He made a gun with this thumb and index finger and, with a wink, shot the Griffin in the mirror.

At a quarter to five he told Jan to hold his calls. The lights on his phone blinked a few times, briefly, while he changed his seat in the room, first behind his desk, then on the sofa, then in both of the big easy chairs. If he sat behind his desk with a script open, would he look too busy to lie? If he sat on the sofa and offered the police the easy chairs, would he look like an arrogant man trying to take advantage of these objects of his contempt? And if he took one of the easy chairs, then Stuckel and one of the cops could take the sofa, but the second cop, in the other easy chair, would be too close. He wanted a barrier, either a desk or the coffee table, in the way of the police. He wanted them together, low, surrounded by fabric.

Jan called him when they arrived, and followed them into the room.

Walter Stuckel introduced Detectives Paul DeLongpre and Susan Avery. Griffin realized he'd expected blue uniforms. DeLongpre was a young forty, with a mustache and shaggy hair. He looked like a baseball player. Avery was a little younger; she wore a light gray suit, and a gun underneath her jacket. She had blond hair, cut like a tight helmet over her ears. Griffin was impressed by the way she let the job dictate her presence. She was a cop. Griffin shook hands with both while Jan asked what they wanted to drink. No one wanted anything. Jan closed the door and gave Griffin a thumbs-up.

Stuckel took one of the chairs, Avery took the next, and Griffin sat beside DeLongpre on the sofa. He felt weak in this position, the police on either side of him. He decided not to wait.

"I'm sorry I didn't call you as soon as I heard that Kahane was dead." Avery began. "Why didn't you?"

"Walter asked me the same question. I wish I had a better answer this time, but all I can say is, it was like running into anyone, nothing special happened. I didn't see anybody following him, he didn't act like anything was going to happen to him, and it was as casual as it could have been."

Now it was DeLongpre's turn. "You went out there just to see him, didn't you?"

"His wife told me he was seeing *The Bicycle Thief,* and I was feeling sort of itchy, so I thought I'd go see the movie, and if he was there, I'd talk to him about a job I was considering him for." Griffin knew June Mercator was not Kahane's wife, but the police didn't correct the slip, and Griffin thought he'd made the story perfect, like a Navajo rug with an intentional error to defeat the symmetry which is only permitted the gods. If he knew so little about the man, why would he kill him?

"You met him inside the theater," said Avery, "and then you went to a Japanese bar, you had a few drinks together, and then he left before you did. Why didn't you leave together?"

"He said he had to go home."

"Why did you stay in the bar?"

"Didn't they tell you about the song? He sang 'Goldfinger' in Japanese, at the piano bar. It was an amazing place and I wanted to check it out. I mean, it would make a great backdrop in a movie."

"Is that what you discussed with him?" DeLongpre.

"Not really, it was incidental."

Avery. "If the scene was so important to you, why did you leave so quickly?"

"They closed up the piano. After that it was just a bar. And I don't drink."

"You drank with Kahane." DeLongpre.

"When in Rome."

Avery. "You didn't know Kahane at all socially, did you?"

"No."

"Were you ever in his house?"

"No."

"Did you know anything about him personally?"

"No."

"Do you think he might have been a homosexual?"

"We didn't get that friendly. Why do you ask?"

Avery looked up from her notes. "Some homosexuals in the neighborhood have complained of attacks."

"Any murders?"

"We thought this might be related," she said, and now the interrogation had devolved into conversation. He was safe.

Walter Stuckel shot his cuffs and slapped the arms of the chair. He was putting on a show, too, thought Griffin. "Maybe we can let you get back to work now."

Avery wasn't so quick to get out of her chair. Griffin wanted to charm her. "Something's bothering you. What is it?" he asked.

"Did you follow David Kahane to the parking lot after he left you? Did you see him in the parking lot?"

"No," said Griffin, "I parked on the street. And I hate to say it, but after this I'm never parking off the street, and if that means getting a cheaper car, maybe I will." He tried to sound lightly shocked, as though he didn't really understand the question. She got up. As Stuckel herded the two detectives to the door, Griffin said, "It was a normal night. That's why this is so horrible. And that's why I didn't call you, I guess. It's scary, it was easier to deal with it by just throwing the newspaper away. I wish there was more I could tell you. I guess if you do arrest someone and you have a lineup, maybe you should bring me in, maybe I'll recognize someone I saw in the theater or on the street. I don't know whether I could connect him to Kahane, but maybe I can help put a puzzle together."

They thanked him and left. On their way down the hall they stopped at a photograph of Glenn Ford, and Griffin closed the door as Walter Stuckel began an anecdote.

Immediately Jan knocked. He let her in.

"This hasn't been your week," she said.

"It was worse for David Kahane."

"I mean this, the postcards, Larry Levy."

"Maybe I've been lucky too long."

"Don't say that."

"In the old days, after the police had been to your office, you'd have a shot of whiskey."

"And now?"

"Now you get back to work." She wanted more from him; he didn't want to give it. Maybe she'll quit, he thought. What would I have to do to make her leave me?

"Well, it's six o'clock," she said, "and I'm going home."

Griffin returned to his desk. He looked out his window and watched the office workers, all on their way home. Some of them were busy all day long, their bosses had ten film posters on the walls, their names on every one, tangible credits, they owned television shows, took calls from millionaire directors looking for good scripts, while others sat by quiet phones and read the trades because their bosses just weren't in the game deep enough, nursing one or two small projects along, encouraged to death by people like himself, Griffin knew, producers or writers making a hundred thousand dollars a year, the salary of a big-city mayor, worrying over an idea that no one really loved, supported, anyway, because the game demanded players. Eventually a script would be finished, submitted, read, rejected, and put into turnaround. Usually the studio demanded a full return on the money it had already spent to let another studio try the story; sometimes it gave the script away for a percentage. Whatever the terms, the script was for sale. George Butler, in the studio's Operations Department, would call the producer who now owned the turnaround and tell him the office was no longer his. The secretary went back into the general pool, or left for a new office with the producer, or was out of a job.

CHAPTER SIX

Griffin woke up remembering David Kahane's funeral. He rushed outside for the *Times* and found the announcement in the obituaries. The funeral was at two. He tried to recall the murder, out of a shudder of respect for Kahane, but the image he summoned, too neat and mechanical, drew him away from what he wanted, a hard connection between the name on the page and the way the name had gotten there. The only reason he wanted to go to the funeral was to see June Mercator. He thought she'd liked him a little, when they talked on the phone, on the first call. Yes, and she'd trickled into his mind a few times, and now he wondered what she was like. Kahane wasn't famous, but he had the glint of someone who lived with a thick-haired prize, a woman with long arms and a wide face, who could look you in the eye and startle you with arcane knowledge. His fluency in Japanese, and the new car, suggested that if he lived in a world partly indifferent to Hollywood—and wasn't June Mercator indifferent to Hollywood?—then she might have a measure for success different from someone who needed Hollywood's approval, and instead of the too eager smile of the wife of a loser—and how many had he met at screenings and parties, commenting on everything, not taking the presence of movie stars or an obviously expensive display for granted?—maybe she'd be quiet and impatient, almost sullen, until she'd decided that the party deserved her best attention, and if it did, she'd be as fun as she'd been on the phone. Well, as fun as she was the first time he spoke to her; she sounded glum and mousy the second time. Of course, he thought, she had a good reason to be low. Her lover was brutally dead.

There was a meeting with the Marketing Department, at two-thirty, but that could wait until later in the day. How long is a funeral? He hadn't

60

been to one in years. When he left for the studio, he still wasn't sure if he'd go, but he wore a dark suit, just in case.

His first call was from Walter Stuckel.

"You did good, boy, you did real good." Griffin knew that the grating effect of the familiarity was intentional.

"Thank you, Walter, I was just trying to be a good citizen, you know?"

"Well, I think you fooled them."

"What does that mean?"

"Something happened out there, didn't it? If I were a Pasadena homicide detective with enough time, I'd find out all I could about young bucks like yourself, and when I learned what a Walter Stuckel knows about them, I'd call you down to the station for another talk."

"And what does a Walter Stuckel know?"

"He knows that young bucks don't hang out in theater lobbies looking for writers."

"Then what do you think happened, if that's not the truth?"

"Did you know he used to be a drug dealer?"

"Really?"

"I checked up on him."

"And he stopped dealing?"

"Who buys anymore? He was small-time, but he'd made enough to collect a few apartment buildings. He made a small killing in real estate. The police don't think this had anything to do with his past. A few years ago it would have been obvious, a drug murder. You don't do drugs anymore, do you?"

"Come on, Walter, I haven't touched a joint in two years, and I've forgotten what cocaine looks like."

"It's white."

"David Kahane was never my dealer. I didn't know the man."

"If you say so." Stuckel hung up. Griffin wanted to say, "I can kill you, too, you know."

He tried to throw himself into work, he returned three calls in ten minutes, said he'd read two scripts and talked to a friend of a friend who'd graduated law school but wanted a non-law job at a studio or with a producer.

Griffin was first in the screening room for dailies. When Levison opened the door, Larry Levy was with him, wearing jeans and a four-hundred-dollar sweater.

"I know he's not supposed to start for a few weeks, but I thought it'd be a good idea for him to see what we're doing now."

"That is a good idea," said Griffin with a big smile, and he stood to shake Levy's hand. He wanted Levison to see that he was already winning. Levy took a seat in the row in front of Levison and Griffin.

The forty minutes of film from the two movies were inconclusive. The footage from Chicago was of a car pulling up to a hotel, and the driver, a minor character, getting out. The footage from the set on Soundstage 12 was all close-ups of a gloved hand opening a drawer.

During the drawer shots Griffin called Jan for messages.

"Joe Gillis said he was confirming drinks, he'll see you tonight at the Polo Lounge. Late, he said, ten."

"Joe Gillis?" said Griffin. "Who's Joe Gillis?" He knew he sounded confused. The name meant nothing to him. Levison snorted and repeated the name at the same time Jan said, "He said you'd know."

"Wait," said Griffin. "You're both talking. Mr. Levison, sir, you first."

"Joe Gillis, that's who William Holden played in Sunset Boulevard. You know, the writer who moves in with Gloria Swanson."

"He said you have his number," said Jan.

Griffin told Jan to cancel the afternoon meeting with the Marketing Department. Now he wanted to go to the funeral. He had to keep making cosmic amends.

"Someone called you and said he was Joe Gillis?" asked Levison.

"It's a friend of mine from college. He'd be a better friend if he weren't so annoying. He's always trying to be smart. Last week he left a message from Monroe Stahr."

"Who's that?" said Levison.

"That was one I knew," said Griffin. "He was the Irving Thalberg character in *The Last Tycoon*."

"I don't get it," said Larry Levy. "This guy calls your secretary all the time using different names, and she doesn't recognize his voice?"

Levison scowled at him. "Let's not worry about it."

Back in his office, Griffin told Jan to call the commissary to have lunch, a salad, delivered. She wanted to know about Joe Gillis.

"I forgot all about it. He's a tax planner my business manager put me on to, he's got a shelter he wants me to buy into."

"I don't think so. I think you're looking for a job at another studio. And I think this Joe Gillis is someone big at another studio, and he's using a code name, and you forgot the code name. Don't give me this line about a tax planner. Would you invest in a tax shelter that was sold to you over drinks at ten o'clock? Why are you lying to me?"

"You're half right. I'm sorry, I shouldn't be playing with you. I don't know any Joe Gillises, it was probably a wrong number."

"I answered the phone saying it was your office, didn't he hear me?"

"Obviously not."

"I don't like the way you're treating me," she said.

"What am I doing wrong?"

"Do you want me to quit? Do you want me to go?"

"Yes, to lunch. Have a glass of wine. Take the afternoon off, get a massage, I'll pay for it. Come back tomorrow."

"I don't want a glass of wine, and I don't need a massage."

"I just get the feeling that you're out of sorts today, and I want to make you feel better." He knew he sounded ridiculous. What was she thinking?

She didn't give in. "So you can treat me badly tomorrow? I'm sorry, but I don't want to sweep this under the carpet."

"Sweep what?"

"Your tone of voice changes every time I come into the room. You sound like you're forcing yourself to be nice to me."

"Maybe you need to take a week off."

"No. I'm fine. I don't know if you understand that, but there's nothing wrong with me. There's something wrong with you."

"Whoa." He held up his hand, to tell her she was pressing too hard, that she was forgetting her place. He waited for her to hide behind a personal excuse.

"It's just that I'd hate to see you crash, that's all." So her tactic was to pretend to be out of control because she was so concerned for him. "I don't want to quit, I like this job. I want you to do well. If you do well, that's good for me."

"Ignore me, then. Don't pay attention to the way my voice sounds. I'm under a lot of pressure, and if I'm taking it out on you, I'm sorry. And I still want you to have a vacation this afternoon." Then he called a salon in Beverly Hills and ordered a facial and massage for her. He charged it to the studio. "Now get out of here."

She stood at the door, and he watched her give in. "I'll have all calls transferred to Celia." She winked and was gone.

He called Bonnie Sherow.

"You can't make it tonight, can you?" she asked.

"Why are we in this business?" he tried to sound weary, like a foreign correspondent, jaded, addicted to bad pay and loneliness.

"Is it over?"

"Not unless you want it to be."

"I don't know."

"What are you doing Sunday morning?"

"What are you doing Saturday night?" she asked, but there wasn't any seduction in the voice; she was puzzled and threatened.

"That's what I meant."

"In that case, Griffin, call me Saturday afternoon." Now she sounded impatient, and annoyed with him. "I don't want to make a date."

"You just have."

"Call me, we'll take it from there."

It was time for a funeral.

He parked a block away from the funeral home and walked toward it on the other side of the street. A stocky, gray-haired man in a blue blazer and gray pants stood in front. Griffin guessed he worked for the mortuary, something about his eyebrows, brought tightly together, and the way he looked up and down the street like a shirt salesman outside his failing store, waiting for a customer. The man studied Griffin for a moment, and Griffin expected him to call out, "Are you here for the funeral?" but the man just looked at his watch and went inside. Griffin looked at his own watch. Two-fifteen. He told himself he didn't have to go in. Then he told himself he did.

The parking lot beside the mortuary was almost empty. He counted fourteen cars. He was surprised to see David Kahane's new Saab; had June Mercator driven to her lover's funeral alone? A few white limousines were parked in the lot, next to the black hearse. And all because of me, he thought. Now he crossed the street.

Griffin slowly opened the door to the chapel, a long beige room. The heavy carpet in the mortuary brought back an old boredom to him, the dull confusion of following his mother through department stores when he was seven. What do they say boredom is, nothing but frustration? Why am I frustrated in here? he asked himself.

The first two rows were full; behind them a few people sat on the aisle. A Japanese family sat in the back. So Kahane's death had brought thirty mourners. Griffin felt himself hating Kahane for wasting June Mercator's time; she deserved a bigger crowd. How could Kahane have expected to make massively successful movies if he had such little charisma? No wonder he'd never had a movie made. No wonder he died so easily.

The door opened behind him and a man in a suit excused himself as he brushed against Griffin's shoulder. He walked slowly down the aisle to the front row and quietly offered his condolences. Two women who might have been June Mercator, mid- to late-twenties, sat next to each other, with an older man, possibly Kahane's father, beside them on the aisle. One of the women had the same thin nose and blond hair as a college-age boy in the row. Griffin figured them for brother and sister and doubted that all of June Mercator's family would be here, making her the single, but then why wouldn't they? If her parents were alive and they lived in Los Angeles and their daughter's mate died, they'd go to the funeral. Would they cross the country for the funeral if Kahane and June Mercator hadn't been married? Probably only one of them would come. The sister could just as easily be June Mercator as the single. Which would he prefer, the sister or the single? Tonight he would have to make the same kind of choice, looking around the Polo Lounge and guessing who was Joe Gillis. He supposed that would be simple; the Writer would be whoever was alone and most self-conscious.

The sister turned and looked back to see the small crowd. She had the bright, functional good looks of a woman who worked in something technical at a studio, a film editor or special-effects artist, with an athlete's haircut, center-parted and longer in back than on the sides, and clear, pale skin. The single glanced back, automatically, to see what caught the sister's attention. Her hair was longer and loose. She had bags under her eyes and she was fleshy. Like me, thought Griffin. She looked tired. From mourning? From her job? He couldn't tell the difference between grief and worry. He pegged her for a lawyer, which made the other woman June Mercator, and that made sense, didn't she do pasteup for a bank's brochures? That's technical. Besides, she was crying.

He let their eyes meet, and he wondered who she thought he was; with so few people there, she was sure to know everyone. His picture had been published a few dozen times, on the front pages of *Variety* and *The Hollywood Reporter*, there had a been a profile in the *Times*, articles in *Newsweek* and *Time*, a picture of him in *Rolling Stone*. Maybe she didn't read those pages. He waited for the small shock when she realized who he was, but it didn't come; she looked past him, then turned back to face the lectern, when a man in a blue suit—Griffin supposed he was the rabbi—stood up to speak.

He talked first about the city, about the horror of daily life, about fear. He referred to physics, to Heisenberg's Uncertainty Principle, and to Einstein, who'd said that God doesn't play dice. Then he said he didn't mean that we should console ourselves that in God's plan David Kahane's death was necessary for the universe to unfold its majestic design, because he knew that David Kahane would laugh at such mindless faith. He said we all had to find meaning in each moment; otherwise, we'd fall into despair. Then he sat down and the college-age boy took his place. He had a sheet of typed notes. He was skinny and clean-shaven, and he looked smart, like a musician, like a bass player, the one who stands to the side.

"My brother," he began, "died after seeing a movie, which I guess is sort of fitting. I hope you don't take this wrong, but I'm glad that he didn't die on his way in, you know, before he saw it. I guess that would hurt me more than this does, and this hurts a lot."

A cascade of disappointment. Kahane's brother looked just like the film editor, so the lawyer with the bags under her eyes was June Mercator. He didn't want to hear any more.

Griffin turned away from the brother and left the chapel. He closed the door as softly as he could. What would the brother think was the reason he left? A surplus of emotion? Or that this stranger had wandered into the wrong memorial service? Maybe he wouldn't notice. Maybe he would think that Griffin worked for the mortuary. You're delivering a eulogy and someone you don't know leaves the room. Disrespect or business? Business. Yes, that was the logical conclusion. And June? What would she think? Now he was sorry he had not stayed in the chapel, and heard the eulogies, learned more about Kahane. He thought of the woman with the bags under her eyes. Could he apologize to her? He would have to be her friend. Was that possible?

He wished he hadn't sent Jan to Beverly Hills. If he called in for messages, Celia would answer and she would tell Levison that he was away for the afternoon. She probably would, anyway. He called Mary Netter, who took the call, and told her that if she and Drew were free, he could see them at five. She muffled the phone with her hand and then came back and said, yes, they were free at five, for half an hour.

When he got back to the studio, he called Celia, and she gave him a message from Mary and Drew that they would not be able to see him. There was no explanation.

He reminded himself that he had a goal: to stop the postcard Writer, to make peace with him. Maybe I should make a deal with one of the other writers I've forgotten. Finish the idea I started with Kahane. Call one of them in, hear what he has to say, and then commit to a first draft.

Whatever the story. A small deal, fifty thousand for a first with a set of revisions. He opened last year's date book and found a few names. Danny Ross; the name meant nothing but gave him a thrill. He went to Jan's desk and found Ross's number. He left a message on Ross's machine. What have I set in motion? he wondered. Will Ross sleep tonight? He'll call before Jan arrives, before nine-thirty in the morning.

There were hours before the Polo Lounge meeting. He tried to read a few scripts, gave up, returned some calls, and went home.

CHAPTER SEVEN

Griffin drove to the Beverly Hills Hotel. He wanted to tell the Writer, "This is probably the most creative thing you've ever done, and I applaud the effort." Had the Writer left his car with the valet, under the pink-and-green roof, or had he taken the cheap way out and parked on the street? Wouldn't the Writer want to avoid a grand entrance? Griffin left the car with the valet, passed a knot of men in dark suits, and recognized a few television executives whose names he'd forgotten. He walked up the long path to the lobby and felt like a millionaire, felt beyond the touch of anxiety.

In the lobby he heard his name called, and turned quickly, in fear, to greet Andy Civella, a rock-and-roll manager, heavy, with a beard, thick hair, and sunglasses. Griffin liked Civella. The manager was a pirate, and after an hour with him Griffin always felt like he did when he'd seen a James Bond film. He was contagiously bold. Civella made Griffin feel invincible and rich. Standing a little behind Civella was Tom Oakley, an English director who had been famous three years ago, that year's boy genius, but two fifteen-million-dollar movies had died, and now he looked tired, a little whipped. Still, he hadn't lost the odor of success. He had the shamelessness Griffin respected; he was in the club. Admire the Writer's strategy, he must have known that Griffin's solitary appearance at the Beverly Hills Hotel at ten o'clock would draw attention. Griffin started an introduction, but they were old friends. He wished they weren't, he was jealous of them, they made each other laugh.

"Join us for a drink?" asked the director.

"I have to meet someone, sorry."

"Another time."

"I'll call you."

"Three twenty," said Oakley.

"What?" said Griffin.

"Room three twenty," he said. "I'll be here for another week."

"Paramount is paying the bill," said Civella with a delivery meant to bring on a laugh and gracefully finish the lobby conference. It worked. Hands were shaken, and Griffin followed the hall to the Polo Lounge.

The maître d' nodded. "Mr. Mill," he said, "how many?"

"There'll be two of us, but I'm a little early."

"Would you like a booth in the back and I'll bring your guest?"

"Give me one in front." And he pointed to a booth against the far wall.

The waiter came immediately. Griffin ordered a shrimp cocktail and a Pimm's Cup, a teenager's idea of sophistication, he knew, but he needed something sweet. Why was he apologizing to himself? Two women at the bar returned his smile. The waiter brought his order.

If he lost the job, what would he miss? He had a lot of his own money, but he wasn't used to spending it, except for clothing, furniture, a few toys. Even his stereo was paid for, a gift of the studio's record company. His expense account was almost unlimited. Every flight was first-class. Limousines brought him to airports and limousines met him. If he didn't know the drivers, there was always a chauffeur with MR. MILL scrawled on a little cardboard sign. In New York he took over the studio's suite at the Sherry Netherland, with his jackets in the closet, shirts in a dresser. He'd flown the *Concorde* ten times. The forty-thousand-dollar car was a gift from the studio. Half his mortgage was paid by the company. An interest-free loan had covered the down payment. When he paid for a meal himself, there was a feeling of novelty, almost of petty theft. But who was he stealing from? How much of the food he'd eaten in five years had he paid for himself? Fifty dinners altogether? Lunches on Sunday? How many plane tickets had he paid for? A few. Cabo San Lucas with Bonnie Sherow. Then he had been a little in love and wanted the hours to be non-reimbursible, non-deductible. So purity had come to this, paying your own way? No. He admitted to himself that this need to pay for his own time went beyond not wanting to turn love into a write-off. It was about privacy. He'd taken no vacations for the first five years he worked at the studio, a record that was even mentioned in *Time* magazine. Well, it wasn't strictly true, on a trip to visit a location in Morocco he stopped in Agadir for three days. He went skiing when a shoot in Colorado was closed by a storm for a week. Two intermissions. In those days he'd thought of vacations as a sign of weakness, a way to recuperate from hatred of the job, from a frustration that came with failure, a compensation. He didn't need compensation. He didn't need weekends.

He watched the maître d' tell a man in a sweater that the Polo Lounge required jackets. The man wore glasses with a piece of adhesive tape holding the temple to the frame. Was this the Writer? The man said he'd go back to his room. No.

The day he lost the job, Griffin knew it would be harder to get the best table, or he'd get it, but he'd have to hang around the bar for a few minutes. Is that it? he asked himself? Is that what it's all about, the best table? All of history, all of power, to have the headwaiter's respect?

The waiter asked him if he wanted another drink. Griffin looked at the empty glass with suspicion, as though someone else had finished it. Whoever it was hadn't touched the shrimp. He said yes, he'd like another drink, and lifted one pink thing from the bed of crushed ice and dunked it into the red sauce.

One of the women at the bar watched him squirt a lemon wedge over the cocktail sauce. He tried not to let her know he could feel her stare, and eating the shrimp became a performance; he was now pretending to be Griffin Mill eating in the Polo Lounge. He wanted to stay in this mode forever, always at a short distance from himself, where he could admire the craftmanship of his being, every gesture, every word, each shift of energy a calculation.

The woman at the bar was not the Writer. She and her friends were great-looking and faceless at the same time, like ten thousand women in town who were great-looking and faceless. Maybe they'd come to Los Angeles to act, encouraged by a small-town photographer, but the movie camera did not love their faces, they were good to the eye, sort of, but in close-up the movie camera detected a numbing symmetry, something ordinary, the fear of revealing—what?—something small, something cheap, an overweening avarice and a fear of the poverty for which they were destined. The women at the bar vibrated with a feeling of complicity for a crime whose silence they were dying to protect in exchange for a big house, a German convertible, facials three times a week. They were all too thin from too much exercise, they needed five pounds more to look human, their creeping anorexia long ago sucked away what might have been most appealing, something to hold on to, something to pinch. The women at the bar used to end up typing scripts in little apartments in East Hollywood, but writers had computers now; no one sent out for typing. What would happen to the women at the bar? Would they ever get married, or married again; they looked divorced, abandoned more likely, by men driven to hysteria after six months cooped up with the lunacy of these fuck baubles. Rich losers. He wanted to leave his booth and join the women at the bar, buy them drinks, and then compel them to the suicides they owed the world. One of them smiled at Griffin. She must have recognized him. If his Writer was a woman, and Griffin accepted the possibility without chiding himself for not having considered it before, she wouldn't have been one of the women at the bar. She would be dark-haired and short, with old sunglasses and no makeup, with the face of a 1925 Berlin Socialist, a serious nose and a mouth that loved talking. She'd wear black, she'd wear flat-heeled shoes, or else she'd be blond and tall and depressed, a brilliant and panicked aristocrat, someone made miserable by interesting men. Women screenwriters did not hang out in the Polo Lounge, they weren't frightened cows. Griffin's private rant subsided and now he felt awful. Maybe these women really were screenwriters pretending to be sluts, out for a night of research. Or not even research, for fun. And what if they weren't writers, only two lonely women. And why lonely? Griffin wanted to apologize for all of his disgraceful thoughts. He wanted to say to these women, "I don't know anything anymore."

No one in the room was the Writer. Maybe the Writer will call me here, he thought, the waiter will bring me a phone, and when I pick up the receiver, I'll hear breathing. Maybe he'll talk to me.

Civella and Oakley rolled into the room, pushing their way past the maître d' and dropping into Griffin's booth.

"So you've been stood up, huh, Griffin?" asked the manager.

"Looks like it."

"She was no good for you," said Oakley. He smelled of marijuana. They both did.

"You guys got stoned," said Griffin, trying to be amiable.

"We want to pitch a story," said the manager.

"The doctor isn't in," said Griffin.

"We'll take it to another studio," said the director.

Griffin laughed. "With my blessings. Let somebody else have the headache."

"No, really," said Civella, "I want to tell you the story now."

"And I don't want to hear it right now," said Griffin, enjoying the tension. The game was starting. He was in the deal flow.

"Back off, Griffin," said Civella. "This is supposed to be fun. It's only rock and roll."

"Wrong. It's the movies. We don't release a hundred albums a year, we make nine movies. There's no margin."

"You've got to relax," said Civella.

Griffin didn't want to fight anymore. "Eternal vigilance is the price of liberty, you know." He tried to smile. "What are you drinking?" he asked, and raised a hand to call the waiter. He ordered mineral water for himself and let them tell the story.

"There's this district attorney who's feeling confused," said Oakley.

"That's not how to begin," said Civella. Griffin saw Oakley curse himself. This was important to him, a rare chance to pitch outside of the studio, catch the executive away from the phone, and he was already messing up and he hadn't really started.

"Okay, try it this way. You're outside the biggest fucking penitentiary in California, the tallest walls—"

Griffin interrupted just to play with Oakley; it wasn't fair and he knew it. "Why California?"

"Because California has the gas chamber. It can be any state with a gas chamber, as long as there's the death penalty, and they don't use a firing squad, lethal injection, or the electric chair. You're outside the penitentiary, with a line of cars going in, and it's night, and it's raining. There's a small demonstration near the entrance, maybe a hundred people, a candlelight vigil."

"Candles in the rain?" asked Griffin.

"Under their umbrellas. The umbrellas are glowing like Japanese lanterns."

"That's nice," said Griffin. "That's a beautiful image. I've never seen that. It's good."

Oakley settled a bit in his seat and picked up his drink. He looked at it, considered a sip, and then put the drink down. "Okay, we're inside one of the cars, and there's a demonstrator blocking the way, a black woman, a real matron, you know from looking at her that she's a good person. This isn't some kind of wild riot, it's very sober. The driver of the car is ready to nudge her with the bumper, but the guy in the backseat tells him not to. Then the woman sees the guy in the backseat, and he lowers his window. They look at each other. Then the car goes in. All right, it's the night of an execution, and the guy we're with is the D.A., who's won the brilliant prosecution of a difficult case and is sending a retarded black nineteen-year-old to the gas chamber." He believes in the law, the crime was awful, there was no question the kid committed it, and now he's paying the ultimate penalty. Which is, by the way, one of the working titles. *Ultimate Penalty.* Anyway, we see the execution entirely through the expression on the D.A.'s face, we hear the sounds of the doors being closed, all the atmosphere stuff, but watch the man responsible for this execution. It's his first. And he doesn't like it. Everyone congratulates him on a job well done, but he hates himself. And on the way out of the prison, he sees the mother in a hearse, leaving with the boy's coffin. At that moment he vows that the next time he sends someone to the gas chamber, they'll be rich, they'll have the best attorney in the state, and he's going to make sure the law is applied evenly. He wants to balance the scales." Now Oakley took a drink.

Civella watched Griffin. "Not bad for a setup, is it?"

"You know it's strong. But it's easy to start strong. Where does it go? I want to hear the story."

"We cut from the D.A. to a wealthy couple in Bel Air, and they're fighting. It's the rainstorm, the same bad weather that they've got at the prison. They go out into the night, he drives away in a fit, she should go with him but doesn't, doesn't want to, there's a witness to the fight, maybe the kids, this part isn't all worked out yet, and then he spins out on a road, and the car goes down a ravine, into a storm drain, and he's drowned with the car, and his body is carried away by the current. When the car is examined, the police find that it's been tampered with, and suddenly it's a murder case, and the D.A. decides to go for the big one on this and put this woman in the gas chamber."

"In twenty-five words or less," said Griffin, "what is the story?"

"Come on," said Civella, "give us a break. We're professionals, you have to hear it all."

"No, I don't. I don't have to hear any of it."

"Then forget about it," said Civella. "I have relationships all over town, and I know ten people who'll sit for the whole pitch. I can think of two who'd give us a commitment based on what you've already heard. You've heard enough, is it yes or no?"

"Call your relationships and ask them if they'll buy a pitch that's only a first act."

"Stop fighting," said Oakley. "I can do it. I'll get right to the third act. First of all, this is a procedural story, and we see a jury deliberating, a D.A. preparing his case, a woman on trial. Of course he wins, and of course she gets the death sentence. While the appeals are running out, something starts to nag the D.A. The body's never been found, that's why the case is so tough, he's sending a wealthy white woman with the best lawyers in the country to her death and he doesn't have a body. And then, the day before the execution is scheduled, he finds out the husband is alive. And now he has to get the husband, and then get a stay of execution. And to make a long story short, the final scene is: The D.A.

breaking into the prison, running down death row and blasting out the windows of the gas chamber after the gas has been released. And at the end of the movie the husband is arrested for attempted murder, and when they ask the D.A. what the weapon was going to be, he says, 'The State of California.'"

Oakley sat far back in the booth and finished his drink, pleased with himself.

"That's more than twenty-five words," said Griffin.

"Griffin, goddamn it, it's brilliant," said the manager. "You know that this is a breakout picture."

He didn't know that, no, he didn't know that at all, but he didn't want to tell them. It was the kind of moral thriller that would appeal to Larry Levy, even to Levison, and if Levy wanted to wrestle with a story that had no second act, and no credible chance for a love story between the D.A. and the accused woman, Griffin would happily let him assume the responsibility.

"Who's going to write it," asked Griffin. "You?"

Oakley spread his hands in a small arc of supplication. "It's my idea."

"We should get somebody else."

"It's his story, Griffin, come on, give him first crack," said Civella.

"It'll cost us too much money. We'll need a rewrite. Don't tell me we won't. You're a wonderful director, Tom, but Levison won't trust you. He'll want someone with a little more heat on him. I'm not saying you won't get story credit, but I am saying that I have to tell you that he didn't like your last film. And I wouldn't tell you that unless I was serious about this story. It has a chance."

"We had a lot of problems," said Oakley. Griffin wished he had blamed himself for some of them. "But this is my idea. I started as a writer. I wrote three plays for the BBC. I can do this one."

"I'll see what I can do. Meanwhile, make a list of top writers you know and can work with."

Civella was about to argue, but Oakley shot him a look to keep quiet.

Griffin excused himself to go to the bathroom. He liked the story, he wasn't sure about the director, Oakley had good ideas and a nice haircut, and he was awfully fun to be with, but after his first movie his style had changed. His casting choices had been weak; it was okay to stay away from movie stars for the sake of balance in the picture, but his ensembles were soft. He worked hard, but his composition and camera angles were uninspired. Griffin would commit to a first draft written by Oakley only if he didn't own the turnaround. It would be hard to beat him on that, but if he held out, the director might cave in. He'd still have points even if he didn't direct it. It was worth a try. He'd give Civella a list of five writers.

When he got back to the table, Civella handed him a postcard of the hotel.

"What's this?" Griffin asked.

"The maître d' said, 'A gentleman asked me to give this to Mr. Mill.'" Civella looked disappointed that Griffin hadn't smiled at the impersonation. "What's the deal, it's a blank postcard."

"Invisible ink," said Oakley. "Invisible ink. That's a good phrase, isn't it? It would make a good title for something, don't you think?"

Griffin nodded, turning the card over in his hand.

"Title," said Civella, "we forgot to tell you the title. It's *Habeas Corpus*. *Habeas Corpus*, is that a great title or what?"

"Go for it," said Griffin.

"I don't like *Invisible Ink*," said Civella. "It sounds too much like the title on a development deal script. It's the kind of title you see on scripts that get paid for but never made. It's not a movie title."

Oakley took the postcard from Griffin. "What's this about?"

"It's a signal from the person I was supposed to meet here tonight. He's telling me that the reason he couldn't have drinks with me was that he's getting laid."

"All that on a blank card?" asked Oakley.

"We understand each other."

"You see," said Oakley, "this proves what I've believed for a long time, that karma is really just coincidence. We're hanging around the hotel with no parties to go to, bored, looking for mischief. You come into the hotel with a purpose. Your friend makes one small change in his night's plans, and now a movie is going to get made, and we're all going to be rich,"

"I'm already rich," said Civella.

"And the agent of all this happiness is . . ." said Oakley.

"Griffin's friend?" asked Civella.

"No. The woman he's in bed with."

Griffin felt himself light-years away from the men at his table. "I have to be up early. Call me at the studio."

"Is this real?" Oakley asked.

"Yes," said Griffin, and he dropped two twenties on the table. "Buy yourselves another round."

"You don't want the receipt?" asked Civella.

"You keep it."

On the way out, he asked the maître d' if he'd recognized the person who gave him the postcard.

"I did not see him. I'm sorry, Mr. Mill. One of the bellboys gave me the card. Do you want to speak to him?"

The bellboy would describe someone who could be anybody. "No," said Griffin, "I know who it is. Thanks." He wasn't sure why, but he slipped five dollars into the maître d's hand. How much money did the Writer give the bellboy? Two dollars?

Griffin gave away another two dollars when the valet brought his car to the front. The Writer was watching him, he knew it. He was either in the lobby, which Griffin couldn't see because of a crowd waiting for their cars, or he was down the driveway, in the darkness, standing in the cover of the hotel's jungle, or he was parked in his car, waiting to follow. Maybe he'll kill me now, Griffin thought. Maybe he has a gun and he'll pull alongside me at a stoplight and shoot me. Maybe he'll force me to go faster and faster up the canyon, trying to spin me out of control, into a tree.

Instead of turning west on Sunset, toward Beverly Glen, Griffin drove south toward Beverly Hills. There were headlights in the rearview mirror, one set that left the hotel at the same time he did, and a few more that joined him at the signal. At the next cross street, in a block of large houses, he made a left without warning, and then drove halfway down the block, to the alley and made another left, into the alley, back toward Sunset.

There were lights behind him. Would the police follow a Mercedes if it turned up an alley? These houses didn't have garage entrances in the back anymore. If he drove quickly, and the car following was the police, he would be stopped. He knew he was shaky. If the police started asking him routine questions, they'd smell the two drinks he'd had and he didn't want to risk an arrest. He dimmed the dashboard light so the glow wouldn't betray his outline to the driver. No reason to be an even better target. He drove at what he thought was a safe shortcut speed, not so slow that he'd be mistaken for someone looking for unlocked gates. Sunset Boulevard was ahead, the traffic at a lull between two red lights. The tail car slowed down, two houses back, and Griffin checked his own speed, so as not to fall into the police's trap.

The two cars stayed at this crawl for the rest of the alley; the traffic on Sunset surged again when the lights turned green. Griffin couldn't burst into the flow, he needed a gap. Now, closer to the brightness of the boulevard, he saw the outline of the car behind him. It was not a police car. The driver reached out, and Griffin saw the gun as it went off. The back window of his car exploded, and there was an interesting delay before the windshield blew out, a section of time in which the bullet was in the car with him, a passenger. Small chunks of broken glass fell from the back of Griffin's head into his collar and annoyed his neck.

For a few seconds neither car moved. Griffin knew that the Writer, frightened by what he had done, was waiting to see if Griffin had been hit. Griffin leaned forward, imagined that he might pass for dead. He pressed the gas pedal to the floor and entered the traffic on Sunset, thinking clearly, proud of that focus. He had been shot at, and instead of collapsing in fear, he had acted quickly; he was now free of a man with a gun, a man who had shot at him, who had tried to kill him. If Kahane had been this strong, thought Griffin, he would have defended himself, he would have beaten me up, or escaped from me and perhaps have run to the police and had me arrested.

The Writer did not follow. Was he crying? Was he blowing his own brains out? Griffin hoped so, but then realized that the Writer's apartment would be searched if he killed himself, and would yield a treasure of unsent postcards, drafts of completed cards, and a diary with lurid entries about Griffin Mill. The Beverly Hills police would visit him, and if no one else put it together, Walter Stuckel would see the parallel between the writer murdered after Griffin had seen him, and the writer who killed himself after a secret correspondence with Griffin.

And here they were, two police cars and a private security company car coming from the east on Sunset. There were more driving north on Rexford, sirens hysterical. Griffin drove east and made a U-turn back toward the alley. He needed to see if they'd caught the Writer. That would be horrible, too, the Writer alive, with a recently fired gun in his car, and an alley filled with broken glass. What would he say? None of your business? They'd put the Writer under psychiatric observation for a few days if he didn't tell them who he was shooting at, and if he did, they'd lock him up and provide Griffin with a guard in case a sharp lawyer got him released. Until the arrest they'd alert all hospitals and emergency rooms to watch for gunshot wounds.

Griffin drove slowly past the alley. The police were out of their cars; a helicopter circled overhead, throwing a hot, white beacon on the scene, as bright as a klieg light at a premiere. The Writer was gone. A man in a dressing gown, the owner of one of the houses, talked to a cop who held a notebook. No one had seen anything, of course, and even with the evidence of the broken glass, there was nothing any one official could do. They'll say it was a mob fight and wait for a body to show up at an airport parking lot in the trunk of a stolen Chevrolet. Or would they know that the glass belonged to a Mercedes?

Griffin turned up Benedict Canyon, in case a police car saw his shattered windows, and headed for home through the back roads between Beverly Hills and Bel Air. He was glad the Writer was free. It was better to live with the threat of assassination than with the Writer in jail and his obsession with Griffin exposed.

The wind inside the car was pleasant, like an island vacation, the ride at night in the jeep from the humid airport to the resort, passing the soldiers with machine guns, when an easy vacation has the feel of adventure. He was away from the Writer, and he turned on the radio. He scanned the dial for an electric guitar. The Eagles were almost right; "Hotel California" reminded him of why he'd moved to Los Angeles, and his early years in town, parties in the hills, drugs, the poignant consciousness of the speed of his success reflected in the self-pity of slower friends. He didn't want the sound of the past. Then he found Van Halen in the middle of the dial. Music to fill an arena, party music for sixty thousand losers. The guitar kept rising higher; was it only an illusion of mastery, a cheap vaudeville, or was it real virtuosity, did it need to be loud to be good? He turned up the volume, and the wind sucked the music out the empty space behind him. He liked taunting the mansions with his noisy wake. If only he could be a guy who makes eighteen thousand dollars a year and lives in someplace unspecific, a town that was like a lot of other towns, where he could be an auto-parts supply-house manager, with a big belly and a truck, dirty ashtrays on the coffee table, a girlfriend with a rose tattoo on her left breast, friends who break into empty summer houses, a long-haired prole who knows that all the power of the universe is here now, because God manifests himself in electric guitars. He wished he could remember riding a bike down a steep hill, arms outstretched, the rush of air, the potential for disaster.

He'd bring the car to a body shop and have the glass replaced tomorrow. With both windows blown out, they'd know what happened. Griffin would tell them a convincing lie.

Not a rose tattoo. Maybe a little map of Texas, or a snake, or a jungle animal. A jet fighter attacking (protecting?) her nipple. The unexpected.

CHAPTER EIGHT

He had been shot at, almost killed, but after his windows were fixed, he couldn't believe that the Writer had ever stalked him. One day he thought he was being followed again, and he took a taxi home from work, but he had to take three cabs that night, to dinner, to a screening, and then home, and another to the studio in the morning. He went back to driving his car the next day.

Danny Ross called at around five the day after Griffin had been shot at. Jan told him that Ross was on the line, and she said his name doubtfully; he must have told her he was returning Griffin's call, but she knew better than to let someone through using that line, it was an obvious trick. Griffin told her to put the writer through.

"Danny Ross!" said Griffin cheerfully.

"Yes, you called?" Ross sounded hesitant.

"When can you come in?"

"For what?"

"I've been thinking about you. You're a talented guy. I'm sorry we couldn't work on that last idea, and I want to hear what else you've got. Or read whatever you've got."

"What idea?"

"The idea you pitched last October."

"I never pitched to you."

"I'm usually the one who forgets." What was Ross talking about?

"No. We were supposed to have a meeting, but you canceled in the morning, I think you had to go to New York. Something like that. And then you never rescheduled."

Griffin looked at Jan's calendar. Ross was right. He had flown to New York to see a play that Levison was interested in, and Jan hadn't crossed out Ross's appointment in the book. Ross's appointment had been on a

Friday, Griffin was in the office again on Monday. Just keep plowing on, thought Griffin.

"Well, Danny," he said, "you've got a good reputation, people talk about you. I heard your name recently, and I remembered it, and I guess I just got confused. When can you come in?"

"What's your schedule like?"

"It's been so long since I stood you up. Why don't you come in tomorrow? You want to have lunch?" Griffin wanted to be as nice as possible. What was Danny Ross thinking?

"Sure."

"The Grill? One o'clock?"

"Sure," said the bewildered writer.

Griffin was supposed to have lunch with two producers. He told Jan to have them come to the office at the end of the week. They were friends, it wouldn't matter.

Griffin worried that Ross would spread the word that he was losing his mind, but it was such a confusing little story, and he was probably overjoyed to get the meeting, get the lunch!, that he'd forget the circumstances. And it was a good time for Griffin to seek peace with the postcard Writer.

The studio was quiet. Larry Levy was skiing for the week in Deer Valley, and Griffin watched the painters working on his office. Old bamboo wallpaper was scraped away, the gray industrial carpet was taken out. Griffin stopped by the day that the color was put on, a dusty peach. One of the painters held a pillowcase next to the wall. The pillowcase was almost the same color. He studied it carefully.

"What do you think?" the painter asked Griffin.

"About what?" Griffin didn't understand the question.

"It's the guy's pillowcase, he wanted us to match it. How did we do?"

"Looks good. What's going on the floor?"

"I hear he wants something red."

Later Griffin told Jan about the pillowcase, and the next day, at breakfast in the Polo Lounge, Levison told Griffin.

"It took me a long time to put my own things in an office," said

Levison. "I was always scared of bringing on the evil eye. I wanted an efficient room, nothing too personal or optimistic. You know what I mean? Even if I'd never have a poster on my walls at home, and I could bring in a nice painting or two, I go with posters in the office."

"So Larry Levy has a different style. I guess I'm somewhere in the middle."

"Well, you like that Southwestern stuff. It's a little precious, but you're a cool guy, you can pull it off."

"And you're saying Larry Levy can't?"

"What I'm saying is, it's a pillowcase. You can be as individual as you want. He asked me if he could make over the office, and I told him if one of his pictures did well, I'd build him the Taj MahLevy. Griffin, if he liked the color, he could have cut a piece of the material and brought it in. But the whole pillowcase. This boy is getting off to a bad start."

"He didn't want to ruin the pillowcase."

"Don't do this to me."

"You can't have it both ways," said Griffin.

"Yes I can."

"If you want Larry Levy to shake things up, you have to go with his style. I think he's being smart. Everything is gray now, or pastel. He wants red, and whether it's strategic or really aesthetic, he's not embarrassed."

"He should be." Griffin watched Levison look at him, and he imagined that his thought was complicated. Now Griffin sounded like the true team player; maybe his deference to Levy's eccentricities signaled his willingness to stay with Levy if Levison was forced out of his job. Griffin saw that Levison regretted an annoyance that was an obvious cover for his own fear of the new kid on the block.

This is all so subtle, thought Griffin. Again he hated the Writer, who must think that we just sit around patting each other on the back, or that when we stab each other, there's a ritual joy to the slaughter, an agreement with the victim. Griffin wanted to push the Writer around, scrape his face against rough concrete walls. How dare you, he wanted to say, try to scare me with your feeble murder attempt when you are dealing with a killer. He wanted to see the Writer dying in the bottom of an elevator shaft, he wanted to stand over the Writer with a big gun and ask him if he knew the difference, at this level of the game, between strategy and taste. Did the Writer understand that for Larry Levy, taste was just one arena to play out strategy?

There was a message at the office that June Mercator had called. What would he say to her? What did she want? Of course, she's calling to thank me for coming to the funeral. It had been ten days. He would apologize for running out so quickly, but he had a meeting; he knew she'd understand.

He called her back. A man answered the phone. He sounded old, eighty. What was he, father, uncle? Hers or Kahane's? June took the phone and then asked Griffin to hold on while she picked up the receiver in another room. He listened while she handed the phone to the old man, and he heard her walk away. Hard shoes on a wood floor. It was an odd sound; what woman wore heels at home, why not softer shoes? Because she was in mourning? Maybe they'd come from the reading of the will. No, luckless writers don't have wills, who wants their shitty old stereos, their small television sets, their record collections with the years they were flush better represented than the years of no money. And their old college textbooks, room numbers scribbled on the inside jacket.

"Sorry," said June Mercator, and the other phone was put back in its cradle in the other room. She was in a quiet room with the door shut, Griffin could tell; she might even be lying down, on a sofa or on the bed. He hoped she was lying down. "I saw you at the funeral."

"I'm sorry I couldn't stay, I had a meeting."

"Don't apologize, please. It's remarkable enough that you came."

"Why?" He said this lightly. He knew what she meant—why would a big-time executive go to an obscure funeral?—but he wanted to be careful not to seem insulted. He hoped he sounded a little bewildered by the question, as though good breeding alone would send him.

"That sounds terrible, doesn't it? I mean, it was nice of you to come, you hardly knew him, you didn't have to."

"He was a rare commodity. He was talented."

"Was he really?" She wanted to know. There was a sound in her voice that carried this sentence: I used to think so, but I started to doubt. If you, Griffin Mill, tell me my man had talent, I'll believe you.

"He needed a break. He needed some luck."

"But he was a good writer. I always thought so. That's why I fell in love with him. His letters, he used to write me letters."

"How long were you together?"

"Six years."

"A long time." Griffin wondered what the call was really about; was there a tactful way to probe? "What are you going to do now?" he asked.

"They gave me a few weeks off from work at the bank. I don't know, go back to work when I'm ready. Actually I'm ready today, but I think that if I go back, they'll be too disturbed. It wouldn't look good, would it? I should wait."

"You do what you have to do," said Griffin.

"But won't everyone think I'm horrible if I go back to work? Don't they want me to stay away? Aren't I a little threatening to them now?"

"Why?"

"I remind them of death."

It was natural for her to call him; hadn't he been the last person to see Kahane alive? That was no small connection. And the short conversation with her, when she'd told him where to find Kahane, hadn't they played with each other so nicely? Friendship was fated. Maybe even love. If he hadn't killed Kahane, would he have pursued this woman, anyway, sight unseen? It could have been a false match.

He was stigmatized too. Jan, Stuckel, the police—wasn't everyone fascinated with him just because he had seen a dead man right before he had died? He would force himself to remember that he was not a suspect when they asked him lots of questions. The questions were natural. Griffin wanted to ask a question. There was really only one thing he wanted to know about June Mercator. The unasked question filled him with a kind of steam; the pressure to ask it grew. He wanted to know if she'd see him. More: He wanted to go to bed with her. But what did he want to ask, right now, ask and be done with questions? He wanted to know if she would go to bed with him. He could never tell Bonnie Sherow he had slept with the widow of the man he had murdered. Not widow, but the same thing.

He heard June Mercator repeat a question.

"I'm sorry," he said, "my secretary just handed me a note." The pressure blocked his ears. It didn't matter what June looked like. It didn't matter if she had bags under her eyes.

"Well, that's all I really called for, anyway, to thank you for coming."

"Business can wait, June." He'd never said her name out loud. It felt odd, stolen, like sitting at a coffee-shop counter and nibbling the food off a stranger's plate. "You were asking me a question."

"I asked if the police had said anything to you, if they knew anything more."

"Have they said anything to you?"

"No, but I thought maybe since you're, well, who you are, that maybe they'll extend some kind of courtesy and keep you posted."

"I'm sorry, no. Maybe they will, I'll let you know, but they haven't said anything, not yet." He drew out his answer. He wanted to keep talking, he didn't want her to hang up, how could he approach her again?

"Well, then, thanks, and . . . good-bye."

"Good luck."

"Thank you." She didn't want to hang up, either, he could tell. It was obvious. They were lingering over the good-bye like two people who've met in a museum and are negotiating the next half hour, that crucial time to have a drink and either say good-bye or mess up each other's lives for six months. It was on his shoulders.

"Keep in touch," he said. He meant it.

"Yes, thank you." End of conversation. Would she?

He tried to remember her face, and improve it if he could. How did she compare to Bonnie Sherow? Thin Bonnie with her long dark hair. She was sort of perfect. She always knew what to wear, she always looked cool and dry, as though she spent her life in air-conditioning, as though nothing were a threat to her. And she had such an aura of competence. What was there to love, really? Once or twice he had seen a gulf between her polished character and something else, as though she were watching herself and wasn't happy with what she saw. In those moments he loved her.

If he had been a girl, what kind of woman would he be now? he wondered. An unloved woman driving a five-year-old Honda Civic she bought used, always the friend, never the center of the story, living in an apartment, all of her friends living in apartments, not knowing anyone who owns a house, saving up all year for a week at a Club Med? Would he become ugly because no one loved him? Ugly like a failed movie?

It bothered him that his thoughts so often returned to Bonnie Sherow. Was it a sign of love? He didn't think he loved her. He owed her nothing, they hadn't even eaten a meal together in weeks, and still he felt like he was cheating on her when he imagined a night with June Mercator. He picked up the phone to have Jan call Bonnie, then dialed her number himself, because he didn't want Jan asking him about her.

Her secretary said she was on another line and asked if Griffin wanted to wait. He said he did. He didn't recognize the secretary's voice; she was new. She must not have known who he was; otherwise, she would have said, "I'll tell her you're calling." He wasn't used to waiting on the phone. The secretary came back after at least a minute.

"She'll be right with you."

Then she was on the line.

When she said hello, he was sorry he had called, her voice was too warm, too happy, to hear from him. The part that was too friendly was stirred by a few molecules of discomfort. She wanted something from him. He thought that this combination of warmth and awkwardness, embarrassment, might force him to marry her, the way two strangers who meet at a wedding buffet and don't particularly like each other but, held in the thrall of good manners, are forced to strike up a certain kind of already familiar, smile-filled conversation and wind up married a few years later.

Griffin said hello to Bonnie. "I just want you to know this isn't a business call. I miss you." He knew he sounded like he was reading his lines. If she felt the insincerity, maybe she'd finally let him go.

"I miss you too."

"It's this business. It's impossible."

"You'll never quit. You love it."

"You think so?" He liked it when he could talk about himself as though he were out of the room.

"Come on, Griffin, you're a natural at this, you know that."

"Yeah, maybe I do." What were they saying? Why?

"I have to go to New York for a while, maybe a few weeks. Can you get away?"

"Not right now."

"When does Larry Levy show up?" Her tone said she was kidding, that he had no competition.

"You think I can't take a break until things are settled with Levy?" He wished he could say, You believe in me, don't you? He couldn't.

"I hear he's painting his walls red."

"The carpet is red, and he's not coming on any way at all, he's skiing. And what's this trip to New York?"

"They want me to see a few plays, and there's a book they'd like to buy, but the publisher is only letting one person into the room at a time, to read the book, and then come back with an offer. Sealed bids, one bid only."

"And the studio is sending you to make the bid?" Suddenly he was jealous of her.

"To read the book. I need to call them before I get a blank check."

"Ohhh," he said, immediately regretting the sliminess of his envy, delivered in a W. C. Fields drawl, but it was too late to stop his sentence, he was falling into it. "So you're back to writing coverage." He meant this to hurt.

"Griffin, that's mean. This is a real responsibility."

"I'm sorry."

"You should be. This is a big step."

"Well then, you have to get the book. It doesn't matter if the movie is made, it doesn't matter if the movie isn't made, it doesn't matter if the movie is made and only three people pay to see it. You have to get the book." He didn't completely believe this, but the compulsion to derail Bonnie's career was too strong. If the studio spent half a million on her recommendation and then had to hire a writer at a quarter of a million, because no one less expensive would do, and the book was unadaptable, too interior, then someone might remember that all that money had been given away because Bonnie Sherow had taken a shot at the first target on the range. Someone would remember. Someone always remembers.

"But what if the book is terrible? What if I think it's a waste of money? Do you know how high the bidding could go?"

"Five hundred thousand." Now he was telling her how much to bid, and he was pretty sure that no other studio would go higher than three. If it was a million-dollar book, they wouldn't send Bonnie Sherow. They'd send someone at his level.

"Wait, why am I telling this to you? You could be in on this. Are you? I can't believe I'm telling you about this. I must be incredibly self-destructive."

"Now do you see why we can't get married?"

"Griffin, is that a proposal?"

He supposed it was. He had to stop this. "But don't worry, I haven't heard anything about a big book."

"And you're not going to go after it now?"

"No."

"We could make a great team." Griffin heard someone else come into her office. Bonnie covered the phone with her hand and then came back after a few seconds.

"You have to go," said Griffin.

"Yes. I'll call when I know I'm coming back, and we'll get together then. Promise. Wish me luck. And thanks."

"For what?"

"For a little strategy." He could imagine the wink that went along with that. The phone call was over. He had made her happy and he had hurt her. Did Levison ever sidetrack him with the same display of affection? Was there anyone in the world whose motives were pure?

And what if she bought the book and the movie was made and it did well? She wasn't strong enough to fight for that kind of credit; her part in the process would be lost in the lights. Or was that only his wish, wasn't she that strong now? Would they have sent her if they didn't have confidence in her? If he was going to marry, ever, wasn't she a good choice? Who else could he marry? He had to marry in the business; otherwise, he would only be half there, and people who married out of the business were admitting failure, were admitting that there was something lacking in their lives. Yes, he thought, success. He could marry an agent, but as long as he was at a studio, his power would be difficult for her; it's easier sometimes to help friends than family. He could marry a lawyer, someone who worked in-house, or from one of the big firms, but he was a little scared of their security; no matter how much authority he had now, he didn't know if he was one of the elect who would run the town when he was sixty, and there was no reason a good lawyer couldn't hang around and just get richer and richer. So he couldn't marry a lawyer because of doubts for his future.

Would marrying Bonnie Sherow be marrying himself, a less aggressive version? Once in a while he would go to a party, or dinner at someone's house, and there'd be a few friends from outside the industry—bankers, doctors, the occasional art dealer. Sometimes there would be a single woman in the group who had been brought there for him to consider. He didn't. He hated to explain what he did, and they always asked. They wanted to know about Hollywood. He resented it when they asked for gossip, he was annoyed by their superiority when they didn't. Maybe it was boredom. They bored him. Maybe he bored them. Of course, they'd been prepped to meet him, and if they were cool, then they saw him as an interesting man with an interesting job, the kind of job held by, what, twenty people in the whole country? Sometimes they didn't know what to talk about with him; maybe they were afraid to talk about whatever interested them. It was just as well, their interests weren't his. They were civilians. He could never marry a civilian. They didn't love the movies the way he did. They asked, "Why does Hollywood make such awful movies, why must it pander to the lowest common denominator, why does it persist in making movies that demean us all?" They liked movies from Europe. They couldn't enjoy an American action movie, but let the Japanese copy a Western and they tripped over themselves adoring it. Creeps. Film buffs. Pear-shaped morons with their shirts buttoned to the collar, whining about the *cinema*. Their fucking *cinema* was subsidized by government television stations; it was all a European scam to pretend to America that someone else had real culture. And their precious little negative stories failed over here the way they failed over there. Griffin saw it all as a giant circle jerk, phonies with prissy taste, with their Saabs, and here he realized that David Kahane was as much of a loser as the Writer, their precious European taste and their precious taste for old movies, against the big virile American public, those millions who create the movie stars, who demand polish, who demand emotional roller coasters, big laughs, big explosions, big tears. He avoided civilians because he'd heard their arguments, and he guessed that the Writer was part of the same nagging mob, people who resist entertainment out of fear that if they like it, they'll be mistaken for slobs. Yes, the Writer was a civilian, he was one of them.

Now he hated the Writer. What are you doing in this business? he wanted to ask him. You don't understand why the audience loves a good silly movie. You think we make them because we're stupid, or that we think the audience is stupid, but you're the one with contempt. What kind of stories did the Writer like? The Writer probably loved film noir. He probably loved shadows and moral ambiguity. He probably hated slapstick, or movies where the audience cries because a wonderful person dies of a disease. Griffin was sick of the Writer, sick of his intrusion into what was already a difficult life. If the Writer wanted to get his movies made, then he had to get past Griffin first, and if he couldn't register on Griffin's emulsion, then he didn't belong. It was that simple. And if he thought himself better than the movies, better than Hollywood, then Griffin wanted the last words the Writer would ever hear to be the player's credo: "I love the audience, I am the audience."

CHAPTER NINE

Griffin walked into The Grill a little after one. He was late. The usual crew of lawyers and agents nodded at him. There was Witcover, who only two weeks ago had screamed at him. Witcover gave a little wave. The room was filled with happy people, millionaires and the men who had helped make them millionaires. The wood-paneled room, with comfortable booths and small tables, was supposed to remind you of old Hollywood; it was supposed to remind you of Musso and Frank's, or any grill from the early twenties, with high walls and pressed tin ceilings. Griffin knew that the Writer would argue that this look was part of the Disneylandization of America, that the whole country was becoming art-directed, that soon there would be no sincere style, that nostalgia was grazing its way to the present. The movies are turning America into a movie, the Writer would say. Griffin knew the argument and rejected it. He liked coffee shops that were little comedies, with waitresses playing the parts of waitresses, and menus pretending to be menus from the fifties. He liked The Grill, which pretended to be a steak joint in old Hollywood; it was a pleasant joke, since none of the new Hollywood people would ever eat a steak at lunch. Everyone had salad or poached fish. No one drank martinis anymore. All the liquor at the bar was just decoration. Why not have lunch on a set? He supposed the Writer would hate everyone here. Of course, the Writer was just jealous.

Danny Ross was already sitting at Griffin's usual table, along the wall, in front. This made Griffin happy. Here was his chance to atone for David Kahane. Ross stood up as Griffin introduced himself with as much charm as he could. He was tall and nervous, the timing of his handshake was off and their grip was uneven, Griffin caught the edge of Ross's palm. He was a few years older than Griffin, maybe thirty-six. Wasn't he a little old for this? Ross had no credits. Why didn't he do something else with his life?

"Let's order," said Griffin, nodding at his waiter. "Have you decided?"

Ross asked for a Cobb salad, lettuce chopped with turkey and bacon. Griffin had the same. Ross buttered a roll, and the dry crust flaked over the tablecloth.

"So," said Griffin, "what's new?"

"In life?" asked Ross.

"No, in the movies. You have any ideas?"

"A few."

"What's your favorite?"

Ross looked down at the table and pressed a finger to the flakes of crust and brought them to his mouth. It was an absentminded gesture. There was something attractive to Griffin in its repulsiveness.

Ross began his story as the salads were brought to the table.

"Your name is Andy," he said. He had obviously told this story before, the pitch was memorized. "You're eleven years old and the last cowboy in America. Everyone else looks into the future, into spacemen and rocket ships and transistor radios, but all that keeps you from collapsing into your nightmares are your beautiful rocking horse, your cactus-and-longhorn bedspread, and an old black-and-white TV show, *The Cowboy*. It's basically the Hopalong Cassidy Show. You know that Hoppy sold three hundred million dollars worth of toys from 1950 to 1955? That's bigger than *Star Wars*."

Griffin already didn't like the story. And Ross was telling it slowly. "So, what happens?" he asked.

"Okay," said Ross. "When the show is canceled, because, as everyone tells you, 'Cowboys are finished,' you're devastated. You watch the last episode, when the Cowboy puts the whole evil Clanton gang behind bars, and then it's over. Well, if it's bad for you, it's worse for the Cowboy himself. His show is off the air, and it hasn't been shot in years. Anyway, the money is gone, he's a big drunk . . . what's left to him but to put on his Western gear one last time and, singing 'Home on the Range,' take a step from an eighth-floor window of a fleabag hotel? And instead of

94

getting the oblivion he hoped for, he's standing at the fence between a desert and the greenest pasture in the universe, the entrance to Cowboy Heaven, where the King and Queen of the Rodeo are really giving it to him for what he's done. When he tries to tell them that the West is finished, they chew him out some more: The West is alive as long as someone believes in it. And he says: 'No one believes in it anymore.' And then they tell him about Andy. Meanwhile, back in the sixth grade, you can't concentrate at school. You try to talk about the Cowboy's suicide, and everyone teases you. One little girl, Sandra, is sympathetic, but you're too broken up to notice. Your nightmares are getting worse. The wolves behind the radiator are on your bed. The Something under your bed is reaching through the mattress. It covers your mouth with its hands, you can't even scream (and if you could, would your parents even come this time?) . . . and then there's a familiar sound of a majestic wonder horse at full gallop, and now the Cowboy is in the room, on his great horse Shadow, and they're cowpunching the monsters, and the Cowboy is shooting the wolves (and can't your parents hear this?), and now the Something melts away, and you're alone in your room with the Cowboy and Shadow. Shadow nuzzles your cheek. 'Looks like Shadow has made himself a friend,' says the Cowboy. This is the hero whose death humiliated you. You start to hit him. And he takes it, because he must. He tells you to get on your pony. You say you only have a rocking horse. He ways, 'Well, then, Andy, rock.' So he gets on Shadow, and you get on your rocking horse, and you start to move, and you can't believe it, but you're entering a blue cloud, the room disappears, and the familiar rolling movement of the rocking horse changes, becomes a frisky bounce, you're out of the room, out of the blue cloud, your rocking horse is now a beautiful little pony, and you're in the West, you're in Cowboy Heaven. And before you can take it all in, breathe the pine air or admire the river and the mountains beyond, a wizened old prospector tears by on a buckboard with the awful news: the Clantons have broken out of jail and they're attacking the stage. Now the Cowboy realizes his mission, to help Andy grow up, and to rid the territory of the evil released by the Cowboy's death. You help the Cowboy stop the stage and capture one of the bad guys, and then he puts you on your pony and sends you back to your bedroom, and your pony becomes a rocking horse again, and when you wake up, you wonder if it really happened."

This was taking too long. Griffin ate his salad slowly while Ross kept going on. He owed it to the Writer and to Kahane to really listen to Ross. Still, there was something inventive about it. If they didn't make the movie, perhaps Ross would be a good choice for an assignment.

"And, of course, you're still not sure it's real, not until you go back when you're not supposed to, and the Cowboy isn't there, and you see the Clantons, dressed as Indians, rustling the cattle, and your pony gets spooked and you fall off. The pony runs back into the blue cloud, into your bedroom, becomes a rocking horse again, and you're stuck. You can't get back. It's real. Now you have to: Walk across a desert. Find the Cowboy. Save the Indians from the angry townsfolk who blame them for the rustling. Save the Cowboy when he's wounded. And you get to: Become Geronimo's blood brother. Fish and play with the Indians. And the Indians' medicine men get your pony back for you, and you finally go home. You promise the Cowboy you won't say where you've been.

Who did Ross imagine would play the Cowboy? If Clint Eastwood wouldn't do it, who was right?

"You've been gone for a month. You don't say where, not until, at school, some kids make fun of Indians in a class play, and you tell everyone what Indians are really like, and how you're Geronimo's blood brother. Then you race home and try to go to Cowboy Heaven, but the Cowboy stops you. You broke the one rule: You told. Then your father burns the rocking horse, which he always hated. Then they bring you to a psychiatrist, who gives you tranquilizers, and you're a dulled wreck. And then Sandra, the girl who always liked you, says, 'Geronimo's blood brother doesn't need tranquilizers,' and she shows you that at night she's a Civil War nurse with Florence Nightingale. You pull yourself together. You teach your father to fish. He knows you've changed, knows something happened when you were away, but he also knows not to press. He respects you. Okay, now one of the kids at school starts a Civil Defense false alarm, and everyone thinks the bomb is on its way, and your teacher faints, you bring order, you lead, you're a hero. And at home that night, content, happy, at peace with yourself, while your parents are having a party and you're in the den watching television on their old black-and-white set, you turn the channels and find, in color, an episode of *The Cowboy* you'd never seen before, but it's not an episode, it's a message: the Clantons have captured the Cowboy. They're getting ready to blow up the train. How can you help? The Cowboy's great horse, Shadow, is in a corral. You call to him and he hears you, and he leaps from the corral and bursts through the television. You get on his back and he jumps through a picture window into the blue cloud."

That's a nice touch, thought Griffin.

"You get a posse, lead the cavalry, and because you're on Shadow, you get to the Cowboy just in time to save him from being blown up. Together you save the bridge and the train, and bring in the Clantons. You even get the reward. And then it's time to say good-bye. The Cowboy takes you to the split-rail fence at Cowboy Heaven. You meet all the great Western heroes. The King of the Rodeo gets your old pony back for you. The Cowboy gives you the reward money. You say good-bye to him. The dinner bell rings. You watch the Cowboy cross the fence, and then you ride away. When you get back to your room, the pony doesn't change back to a rocking horse. Your parents are there, but they can't really speak. You casually give your father all the gold coins from the reward. You ride downstairs and out to the bus stop. You put the kid who always tormented you in his place, and then you ask Sandra if she wants a ride to school. She gets on. The pony carries the two of you away, and you ride into the day while Roy Rogers and Dale Evans are singing 'Happy Trails.'"

Ross put a wad of salad into his mouth and waited for Griffin to say something.

"This is the best idea I've heard in a year and a half," said Griffin. "We have to get it to Spielberg." He was honor-bound to make this Writer as happy as possible, and to get him the deal. He was honor-bound to make *Cowboy Heaven* and stop the postcards. "One question, though," he said, watching Ross contain his triumph. "Does it have to be the fifties?"

"I thought of setting it in the present. Andy tapes old Westerns at three in the morning."

"Good," said Griffin, "in case people think the fifties have been done to death."

"The audience always likes it," said Ross.

"I want to chase this one," said Griffin.

Sylvester Stallone came into the room with his agent. The agent stopped at Griffin's table. Griffin knew Stallone. He introduced Danny Ross to him. "Sly, this is Danny Ross, the Writer." Stallone's agent looked Ross over; obviously he was important, but why hadn't he ever heard of him? Calling him the Writer was a good touch. Griffin could see by his stunned silence that Ross had just been airlifted to the top of K2.

As they left the restaurant, Griffin asked Ross who his agent was. Griffin knew her, Marla Holloway. He told Ross to have her call. They said good-bye. Griffin handed his claim check to the parking attendant, and Ross walked away, into Beverly Hills. Of course, he had parked at a city lot. Of course, he could afford the three dollars for the parking; he just didn't want anyone to see whatever kind of awful car he drove. What did Danny Ross want to drive? A Honda? A lot of writers drove them, thought Griffin. Prissy people. Griffin's Mercedes came to the curb, and he went back to the studio.

When Griffin first came to work at the studio, reading scripts and writing the coverage on them, Levison was the hero to a hundred hopeful executives. The studio's guiding principle had long been to hire movie stars and directors who had won or been nominated for Academy Awards. Levison was the studio's wild card. It was said of him that the studio didn't understand him but was too scared to let him go. Young comedy directors, young horror directors came to him, and he argued their stories in court, and their movies were made. After the then head of production spent thirty-five million dollars on a flat musical, the studio's chairman fired him, and in three days Levison was in charge. The predecessor left the studio with his two vice-presidents, from whom he was never apart, and Levison was free to fill the offices in his hall. Watching him, Griffin thought he'd recognized a calculation supporting each part of Levison's behavior, which was relaxed, almost careless. Levison was always a little sloppy. He needed a haircut, or his tie was uneven, and his car was a dump for scrap paper, old scripts, newspapers, and parking passes. Where was the strategy in that? Now no one else could be messy.

There were other executives to mimic, but Griffin saw that those newcomers who copied the more flamboyant styles looked obvious. Griffin hated shaving, but he knew he would never grow a beard. Some very rich men in Hollywood were bearded, but most of the assistants and vice-presidents who wanted to look like rich producers with beards only looked like those assholes with license plates frames that say MILLIONAIRE IN TRAINING or MY OTHER CAR IS A PORSCHE. The bearded producers were only copying the bearded directors. The bearded directors were all copying Francis Ford Coppola. And Coppola, Griffin told himself, was too busy to shave, or didn't like the shape of his chin. Levison encouraged a casual style at the studio, which his executives appreciated, because this slight contempt for expensive, impeccable grooming gave them a feeling of belonging to the team. From a distance Griffin watched Levison and admired him. Levison, before his promotion, had let it be known that he liked Griffin's script reports and had, a few times, asked him into his office to talk to him about movies, about casting, about directors. Griffin knew he was being scouted for a position, and one day, after his promotion, Levison asked him to sit in a meeting with him, when a director whose fee was three million dollars came in to pitch a story. After the pitch Levison turned to Griffin and asked him what he thought. Griffin had said, "This is not a finished idea." Levison said nothing, the meeting ended, and when the director was gone, Levison told Griffin he was now a vice-president. At that moment Griffin had fallen in love with Levison; the feeling of relief and pride had overwhelmed him.

Then he understood that Levison's cultivated eccentricities were not without purpose, that he used the bits and pieces of his personality as weapons. After he was hired, Griffin always walked away from the crowd when people did Levison impressions, the head cocked just so, the brow furrowed before asking a difficult question, the repeated phrase, "I submit . . ." As in, "But I submit that you could shoot these three scenes in one location, and if you could, then why do you need the second two?" Griffin hoped that people made fun of his own manner, but he knew they probably didn't. If they do, he thought, then I probably have a better chance of being head of production someday. It was, he knew, too late to develop a trait for the sake of attention and power. He wished he was marked, or scarred in some way. He reconsidered something. Of course, there was a Griffin Mill impression, and it went like this: "Let me think about this for a few days. I'll get back to you."

Griffin was in a meeting with Aaron Jonas, an agent who wanted to move into production, when Jan called him on the intercom to say that Andy Civella was on the line. Griffin excused himself and took the call.

"So, are you ready to pitch?" he said, trying, with his humor raised, to anticipate Civella's attack of confidence.

"I already pitched. I'm waiting for your response." But this wasn't Civella.

"Andy?" Griffin asked, but it wasn't Civella. Who knew he had seen Civella? He knew it was the Writer.

"I think I'm just going to haunt you. I want to make you uncomfortable. I want you to be so distracted that it's impossible for you to work." Then he hung up. When the Writer was at the Polo Lounge, he saw him with Civella, had recognized Civella. Why be surprised at that? Civella was a little bit famous.

"I'll call you back," said Griffin. "I'm in a meeting with Aaron Jonas." He covered the mouthpiece with his hand. "Aaron, do you know Andy Civella?" Aaron shook his head no, but of course knew who he was. Griffin continued talking to the Civella who had never been there. "Aaron's a good guy. I should get the two of you together." With that needless charade, Griffin put down the phone.

As Aaron talked on about the kind of job he wanted, a creative department job in a studio, a job that would lead to independent production, he didn't want to stay in an organization, which was why he was leaving the agency. Griffin listened to his voice. Griffin tried to separate the sound of Aaron's voice from the words, tried to compare this voice to the Writer's. It was a winner's voice, not so much rich as solid, each word was said quickly, but not clipped, there was no hesitation, and none of those little squeaks that betray conflict, unhappiness, and fear. It was a voice Griffin heard every day, lawyers, agents, directors, free of deprecation, sometimes conveying arrogance but usually only as a negotiation tactic. It was the voice of the Players of the Game. The Writer did not have this voice, this successful voice. The Writer was not a Player. How had he said, "Impossible for you to work?" With a whine he acted the sentence. Griffin heard the rehearsal in the delivery, and there was a sneer, a sound of self-satisfaction, inappropriate because he assumed power. He had no power . . . well, only the power to kill Griffin, or to embarrass him, perhaps.

Did the Writer know that men like Aaron, who he would surely despise for his smugness—and Aaron *was* a bit smug—were sometimes not satisfied with their successes? Griffin's private defense of Aaron, against the Writer's contempt, made Griffin, who until now had never thought of Aaron as someone of whom he could expect great things, suddenly wish the best for him. Griffin told Aaron he would keep his ear to the ground, and he meant it. He saw that Aaron knew that Griffin would look out for him, and when they shook hands, Griffin was glad to see his friend's confidence and excitement. Aaron had such an easy way with himself. To be superior without contempt! Tonight Aaron would tell whoever he was having dinner with that Griffin Mill was on the case.

Later that afternoon Jan told him it was Andy Civella on the line. He thought of picking up the phone and immediately screaming at the Writer, but what could he say to scare him? It was the real Andy Civella.

"We're ready," said the producer. "When can we come in?"

Griffin looked at his book. "How ready are you?" he asked.

"Come on, Griffin, Tom Oakley and I are ready to say that if you don't give us a meeting this week, we go to another studio. And you know I don't want to. Because, because . . . I love you, Griffin." Civella laughed. Griffin recognized the rhythms of other people in Civella's humor, there was a lot of Eddie Murphy, and sometimes a maniacal screech that was someone else's trademark, and currently popular among comedians who worked the comedy clubs.

Griffin looked at his schedule for the next two days. "How about tomorrow afternoon?" He heard Civella's breath change, it registered defeat, he had to say yes, but it would mean he now had to make a difficult call to cancel something important.

"Five o'clock," said Civella with a casual lilt, as though he were echoing Griffin.

"I'll see you at four," said Griffin. "And really, I can't wait." He didn't care if Civella thought he meant it, and he wasn't sure, and it didn't matter.

He watched the lights on his phone. There were five lines, all for him, so that no one calling would get a busy signal; he wished he understood the circuitry. How did a call coming to one number get bumped to the next number if the first one was busy? How did the hold button work? What is hold? he asked himself. You have a caller on line one. Then a call comes through on line two that can't be left hanging, so you push in the hold button when you excuse yourself to the person on line one, and then that light blinks while you talk to the person on line two, and anyone studying the lights on another extension on the circuit can tell by the pattern of blinking and clear lights which lines are on hold and which line is engaged. There's even more mystery to the circuitry. Griffin counted all the phones on his line. There was one on the desk, one on either end of the sofa, and one in Jan's office. Four phones, five lines, all connected to one number, with supplemental numbers that made it possible for each phone to be used independently, four people could make calls out of the office at the same time, and still one person could get through, and all four calls could be put on hold while the four callers could each talk to the call coming in. How? Some people knew exactly. Somewhere brilliant people, electrical engineers, computer geniuses, mathematicians, physicists, too, probably, had, over the course of a hundred years, added the increments of knowledge and research and surely even some luck and intuition to create this immense circuit. This was the kind of thought Griffin wished he could share with Levison, without making a meal of it, to mention, idly, how wonderful and complicated the phone system is, how we take it for granted. Maybe they could then move on to the broader implications of this small, admittedly obvious discovery. And what's wrong with the obvious? thought Griffin. How much that we call obvious have we really stopped seeing? Maybe it was obvious once, but since then it's changed. What would Levison say, that Griffin sounded like he was talking about the need to stop and smell the roses? Well, Griffin knew he could say yes to that, without apology. What we love are patterns, flowers, phone circuits, familiar stories. Griffin knew he wouldn't say anything, wouldn't even think about the phones the next time he was with Levison, in case his whole tortured elegy came out compressed as, "Phones, pretty amazing."

He wanted to call June Mercator. He wanted to see her, to impress her. This came to him as a desperate longing, and he saw that this call from the Writer made him need the woman he had made a widow; he wanted June Mercator.

He called Jan to set up a few minutes with Levison. She put him through to Celia, who put him through to Levison. "I just heard a pitch," said Griffin, "and I think that if we don't grab it, someone else will."

"Let's hear it first."

"There's this little kid—it's 1957—a ten-year-old boy who's totally obsessed with a kind of Hopalong Cassidy figure whose show gets canceled. The old Hoppy figure kills himself, but instead of going to hell, he goes to Cowboy Heaven."

Levison interrupted him. "A forty-year-old man and a ten-year-old boy, right?"

"It's more than that."

"And there's a trip to the West, right?"

"Yes."

"Forget it, I'm allergic to horses. Anything else?"

"No," said Griffin.

"Well, all right, then."

Jan buzzed to tell him that Marla Holloway was on the line.

"Hello, Marla."

"Oh, Griffin, I'm so excited. Isn't Danny just terrific? And isn't *Cowboy Heaven* the best idea you've ever heard? And I think giving it to Spielberg is a brilliant idea."

"Marla, Levison didn't like it. I'm sorry. I'll have to pass."

"Why not send Danny to see him?"

"Marla, no. It won't work. Tell Danny I'm sorry."

"He has some other ideas," said Marla. "You should hear them."

"I'm busy right now, Marla, I'll let you know when I'm free."

He had done his best, and Levison had passed, and that was his right. This lunch had taken time, he'd canceled with people who really counted. He had killed, too, and still the Writer plagued him. Well, then, forget the Writer, he thought. He would let him call or not call, write or not write, shoot at him or not shoot at him, but Griffin would not look for the Writer, send oblique messages to him in *Variety*, make mental contact through the ether, or let his thoughts dwell on him, even negatively, as in the children's game when one says, "Don't think about an elephant." He could beat any child in that game, he knew how not to think about the elephant. It was easy. All you had to do was work hard and think about what was at hand.

He called June Mercator. Her machine answered. He had ten seconds to decide if he would leave a message or hang up.

"This is Griffin Mill," he said. He didn't know what else to say, but he couldn't retreat now. If the machine was voice-activated, and he didn't say something quickly, then it would think he had hung up, and his message would sound wrong, cut-off. He had to be sure of himself with June Mercator, no hesitation, nothing awkward. "Call me at the office if you can, and if you can't, here's my home number."

When he hung up, he wondered if she would be excited by owning his home number, such an intimate gift. No, she would think he had some news about David Kahane, she would think he had spoken to the police. He had stumbled on the dance floor, when she called back, she would be thinking of the man he had killed. He hoped she would call late. The later the better; he would sound tired, a little sleepy, too comfortable in his bed to maintain the forward manner of the proper executive, he would speak quietly, with a little extra huskiness, letting her know that he brought luck to those who were near him; he would start to seduce her.

Levison called him to a crisis meeting, a director had broken a leg and a replacement had to be found. Griffin got on the phone in Levison's office and started calling the big agencies. He had a mission: find out who was good, who was available, who would go to work in three days, someone who would accept a fair price and not involve anyone in the usual negotiation quadrille. If Larry Levy had not been away, Levison would probably have called him, Griffin knew. Here was a chance to show off. With Levison watching him, Griffin was negotiating a director's fee in ten minutes.

CHAPTER TEN

That night he went to dinner at Morton's with an Australian producer. A few heads turned as Griffin walked to his usual table, by the wall. He shook hands, was introduced to a wife. People smiled at him. Andy Civella was at the bar, and when he saw Griffin, he came to the table.

Griffin introduced him to the Australian.

"Don't forget tomorrow, Griffin, don't cancel." Then he turned to the Australian. "How many times did he set a date for this dinner?"

"This is our second attempt, but I had to break the last one."

"Then you're a bigger deal than he is. We should do business."

The Australian blushed. He was confused. Civella took charge.

"Listen, I can get away with this because basically I'm rock and roll."

Levison and his wife came in with Ted Turner's lawyer and took the table behind Griffin's. Levison understood that Griffin's dinner was business, so he skipped the usual two-minute chat.

The Australian wanted the studio to help finance five movies over two years, and the studio was interested. It was Griffin's job to talk about stories and casting, to make sure that the Australian wanted to make movies that a lot of people would like, that his characters were big enough for movie stars, that they would triumph absolutely, that there would be no ambiguity. Griffin thought about Larry Levy, who was coming back to a shop he was sure was waiting for him, and decided that he had to commit, now, to the Australian, and then, tomorrow, to Civella. He knew that Larry Levy expected Griffin to stop work until the dust had settled before starting new projects, and he also knew that the Australian would set up house somewhere else if Griffin didn't start a deal with him. Did it matter if the deal never went through? Negotiations would likely take three months. The thing was to unsettle Levy.

When they shook hands in the parking lot, the Australian knew he was in business. Griffin watched him drive away in his rented car, and then went home, thinking now only of his answering service and if June Mercator had called.

She had called a little after nine, and the message from her was to call whenever he got in. So he had alarmed her. This made him think about the Writer, the next association after a quick stop on David Kahane, but he let the intrusive thought slide into the same memory chute that he'd put some random image of a building he hadn't seen in twenty years, or a particular day at school, one of those pictures that come back sometimes in idle moments and then disappear.

It was now ten-thirty. He began to dial her number, then put the phone down. He took a shower, started to shave before he realized it was night instead of morning, but finished the job, anyway, got in bed, turned on the television, watched a few minutes of news, and then, a little after eleven, he called her. She answered the phone knowing it was him, there was no panic about a late-night call. Maybe she stayed up late, maybe she and her friends called each other at midnight all the time. He doubted it.

"I was out all day," she said. "Some friends took me to the museum and then dinner. Do you have news?"

He was ready for this. "No, I'm sorry. I was wondering if you had heard anything."

"No."

He had to move quickly, he had to fight feeling like an ugly fifteen-year-old calling the prettiest girl in the class. "I just wanted to tell you that whenever you feel like it, give me a call, just to talk." If he said any more, he'd sound nervous. Until she gave him a clear signal, he would ask for nothing more. It was strange enough what he was doing, from her point of view. Was he a leech taking advantage of her tragedy? Or did she think that this was dangerous and thrilling? With an undeniable current between them, could she give in to it now, with David Kahane only recently dead, and open up a new territory of desire and permission?

"I will. Thank you."

He went in for the kill.

"Where did you go, the County or the Contemporary?"

"Just the regular collection at the County. They have some nice paintings from the Hudson River school."

It was time to show off. "I don't know if it's politically correct, but I'm a real sucker for nineteenth-century landscape."

"Your secret is safe with me," she said.

It was time to probe. "Have you been back to work?"

"Yes, I couldn't stay away. It's been good. Everyone's been incredibly nice to me."

Griffin put the phone on the pillow and rested his head on it. He was sleepy. "What are your plans?"

"I don't have any."

"Look, I'd like to see you. I don't know if that's possible, I don't know you, I don't know what your life is like, I'm sure you've got good friends who can help you through this a lot better than I can, but I think there's a connection between us and—" He stopped, to give her a chance, to let her finish his sentence.

"It's difficult. I don't know exactly how I feel right now. But there is a connection, and I would like to see you. The night you called, to speak to David, I had a feeling about you, that I'd hear from you again. I suppose that's awful to admit, but I've learned a lot from this"—she meant the brutal murder of her lover—"and it's important to say what you feel. You can't find out what you really feel until you just start admitting all your feelings. And those feelings change. Oh, God, I'm running at the mouth, aren't I? Well, I'm not going to apologize."

He thought he should turn the tables on himself, make himself a victim of this situation, try to say that it would have been easier calling her behind David Kahane's back than over his dead body. He tried it this way: "It would have been easier calling you if he was alive."

"Yes."

"But I called you, anyway."

"I'm glad you did."

"It's easy talking to you. Is it easy talking to me?"

"Yes."

"There's a lot we aren't saying. But I'm proud of our restraint."

"It has a certain elegance, doesn't it?"

He didn't want to go any farther yet. "Good night," he said.

"You too."

Whose move was it now? He would call her in a few days and make a date for the next weekend. He had forgotten what she looked like. He would know her if he saw her, but he could not describe her. Dark hair, sad eyes. He turned off the light, and out of the pulsing darkness of his room he tried, but failed, to create a picture of June Mercator. All he could conjure of her was a shape, arms reaching out to hold him. He closed his eyes, and in his own darkness the shape defined itself a little more; now it had long hair. It hovered, waiting for him. He could stroke her thighs. The shape would not come closer. Maybe I'm just blind with desire, he thought. I can touch but I can't see. He knew that in her room June Mercator was playing with a projection of him. He rolled onto his stomach to tease the shape closer; he didn't want to stare at it and frighten it away.

He expected to find a postcard with his newspaper in the morning, but there was nothing. He had breakfast at the Bel Air Hotel with a director.

As soon as Griffin settled into his office, Larry Levy knocked on the door with a hard cast on his wrist. The sun- and windburn on his face stopped around the shape of his goggles. Griffin knew Levy wanted to talk about the broken arm, how he'd hurt himself, what the doctors had been like, so he didn't ask about it when he invited him to take a seat.

"Welcome back," he said. "Your office is finished?"

"They did a beautiful job. I'm very happy." He took an emery board from his pocket and scratched inside his cast. "It's time to get to work. Levison is giving me a few projects. A couple of books they've bought, and a few ideas for remakes. He showed me his writers list, and I told him I didn't like it. I don't want to be confined to the writers he trusts."

"If you like someone, you can always argue his case."

"And directors too. We need more interesting people. We shouldn't do business with anyone who's ever directed a Neil Simon movie, for example, and there's three of them on the directors list."

"Who do you want to put on it?"

"Well, that's the point," said Levy. "We have to find them. Young directors, hip directors."

"You mean, we should go to the film schools," said Griffin dryly.

"Exactly. And to the festivals too. And I know what you're thinking, everyone does that, but the point is, we have to be smarter about talent. And I think I have a good eye for talent."

"You've said all this to Levison?"

"Of course."

"And he bought it?"

"What is that supposed to mean?"

"Whatever it sounds like."

Griffin had to pick a fight now, had to keep Levy nervous. "You mean, we shouldn't find talented new directors who have a new approach to movies?"

"I mean, the audience doesn't care, really. It's true there's lots of hacks, but even the hacks can turn in a hit if the script is right."

Griffin didn't know if he believed what he was saying, and he could just as easily argue against himself. He needed to voice the slightly perverse opinion, even if it was the easy critique of the self-declared outsider. Since Larry Levy had Levison's blessing, whatever he'd say would be the company line, and Griffin knew that unless he was different, and strong, he was out. Maybe he'd be out, anyway, but he couldn't parrot Levy. The obvious course was to put on a grin and agree with the new executive. Maybe he could shake him up in private and agree with him in public. Anything, so long as Levy couldn't predict Griffin's next move, his next thought. If Levy came to hesitate whenever Griffin was nearby, Griffin would quickly crush him.

Levy scratched inside his cast again. Something itched him fiercely, and still Griffin refused to ask what had happened, how he had fallen on the slopes. He sensed that Levy knew Griffin was purposefully ignoring the cast, waiting for Levy to offer the explanation, which would, because it was volunteered, carry the unmistakable whine of the victim. The urge to tell the story of how he broke his arm was a second itch. "Look, Griffin, I think we're getting off to a bad start here."

"I'm just trying to see where you stand. We have different philosophies, and I think it shows good judgment on Levison's part to bring you in. If each of us is right just once this year, and we manage to get a couple of movies made with our own strategies, then we both win."

"They have to be hits."

"Yes, that too."

Larry Levy scratched again. "Gee, this itches. Do you ski?"

"Don't have the time anymore."

"Some guy ran into me on a steep slope, and I did an eggbeater down the hill, and along the way I snapped my wrist."

"Well," said Griffin, not asking him to explain an eggbeater, trying to be as unsympathetic as possible, "you'll be too busy for sports for quite a while."

Levy stood up from the uncomfortable chair. "Let's work together, Griffin. Life's too short." He held out his left hand, since his right was in the cast.

"Of course," said Griffin, thinking of David Kahane. He took the offered hand and pressed it. If Levy said anything else that was conciliatory and emotional, Griffin was going to come back at him with a crack about not making a habit of ending every meeting like the last song at a campfire. Levy didn't say anything, which was just as well. Bury the sarcasm, save the impulse for moments of real cruelty. If not intentional cruelty, at least an action developed from such intense self-interest, or corporate interest, that no one would quarrel with the need for the attack on whoever is taken as a threat, only with the heat of the response. From now on he should pick on Levy in meetings. He needed witnesses. They should envy the cruelty. Griffin wasn't sure whose envy he meant, those below him or those above him. An act of distinct cruelty should make those below jealous, or even sick of the business; it didn't matter which, so long as they understood that in that recognition of their lack of stomach for the job, they admitted their acceptance of a limit to their own ambition. As for those above, well, of course they should recognize a member of the club.

CHAPTER ELEVEN

Jan called him and said that Susan Avery was on the line. "Who?" he asked. From Jan's tone he knew she expected him to recognize the name. She said the name coldly, she must have been important, but why?

"Detective Susan Avery, Pasadena Police. Remember?"

"Of course." It was time to draw up a list of all the names he had to keep track of. Really? No, it was the sort of scrap that becomes evidence.

"Should I tell her you're not in?"

"Put her through."

There was a pause, and then Griffin said, "Is it Officer or Detective Avery?" Would she say, You can call me Susan?

"Lieutenant, actually. Detective's all right."

"How can I help you?"

"Well, I was wondering if you could come to the station."

Griffin couldn't tell if this was a trap, and if so, should he tell her he needed to speak to his lawyer, or was she asking him to come down to look at mug shots, in which case mentioning a lawyer might tip her to his panic, and so far he had been so calm with her. Or would she expect him, in his role as important executive, to demand his right to a lawyer? In her eyes he was hardly a common citizen. How far was his free cooperation expected to go?

"Have you caught the killer?"

"We'd just like to ask you a few more questions."

He had to go. He knew he had to hesitate a little. If he was innocent, how would he act? Annoyed at the intrusion, or curious about police procedure? Would he make a mild joke, or would that be in bad taste, or would the detective appreciate it? After all, he had no connection to the dead man, and the police weren't in perpetual mourning for every corpse whose death they tried to solve.

"You understand, I've got a studio to run." He looked at his calendar. He could skip dailies. "I can come down in an hour, for about half an hour, or not until the day after tomorrow."

"An hour?" Now it was her schedule that needed juggling. "We'll see you then." She gave him directions.

He called Dick Mellen. What does an entertainment attorney know about the police?

"What's up?"

"We're having a debate on a point of law. Actually, it's not a point of law, it's a point of police procedure. If the police suspect someone of murder, but they don't want to tip their hand and they ask to interview the suspect, do they have to tell him his rights so he can bring in a lawyer?"

"Griffin, please, contrary to popular opinion, I am not a criminal lawyer."

"And the script may go into turnaround. I'm just trying to figure out if the scene is believable. I don't know whether the audience would buy it."

"I think that the police would have to let him bring a lawyer. But maybe not. They don't want him to know he's a suspect?"

"Right."

"You know, the Supreme Court has changed things so much in the last few years. Look, if the scene would be better without the lawyer present, keep it that way. *I* won't complain."

"Thanks." So they probably did have to let him have a lawyer there, which meant they didn't suspect him.

He drove through Glendale to Pasadena, up the hill that led to the San Gabriel Mountains. The air was ugly, and the sunlight was fluorescent, and it made him wonder why anyone would live in this part of the world if they didn't work in the movies. If he didn't work in the movies, he would live in Seattle or San Francisco, or even northern San Diego County, where the ocean was clean and there didn't seem to be a lot of pressure to be famous. There was a town, Leucadia, with a nice beach and a café where folksingers played on the weekends. He'd been there once when a film was shooting at Camp Pendleton, not far away. If he had to live in L.A. and he wasn't in the movies, he would live near the beach. He had lived in Malibu for two years but moved back into Beverly Glen because he hated the long drive. There was no human reason to live in Glendale or Pasadena.

He was fifteen minutes late to the police station. The policeman at the front desk took his name and told him to wait. Perhaps this would be the limit of his punishment for murder, pulled from his desk for a few hours, forced to answer a few questions, sent back to the studio in heavy traffic. And if Susan Avery had lulled him into coming to the station without a lawyer because she wanted to humiliate him with a public arrest? Griffin decided that he had to enjoy himself now; he was alive and he was free. In minutes his freedom might be over. What kind of bail would they set for him? Fifty thousand dollars? A hundred thousand dollars? A million? There would be headlines, it would be front-page news. Bonnie Sherow would support him. He would tell her he was innocent and she would believe him. June Mercator would be horribly confused. Would she believe in his innocence? He hoped so, but she had no reason to support him. Walter Stuckel would know he was guilty, but would he keep that to himself? He would talk about it with his friends, in a wood-paneled den somewhere in Northridge or Thousand Oaks, in an old house he couldn't afford now if he tried to buy it at market price. And Levison? Levison would offer any help. The studio couldn't pay for his lawyer, of course, but he would be offered private support. Larry Levy would be happy. Levy would say he was guilty. If Griffin were in Levy's shoes and saw his rival arrested for murder on what appeared to be thin evidence, and he wanted to insure that this hurt him at work, he would convince Levison that in the studio's best interests as a publicly held company, an officer of that company, accused of murder, should withdraw from active duty until the resolution of the case. Salary wouldn't stop, but responsibilities would. Levison would resist, for a day or so, but by that time someone on the board of directors would call him, and ask about the case, and say what Levy had said. Levison would see that prudence was wisdom. Levison would doubt Griffin's innocence the moment he had to ask him to leave, when his shame, for caving in to expedience, turned to anger at his own weakness. Levison did not like to think of himself as weak. He wasn't weak. Griffin knew Levison had no trouble firing people, and that his reflex emotion after a large studio layoff was disdain for the fired workers. After asking Griffin to leave the studio, he would never respect him or fear him in quite the same way. Did he fear him? Probably. Otherwise, he would have fired him before bringing Levy aboard.

Griffin looked at the people around him. What if he assembled a panel from them to discuss his current problems. They could never understand. They would say, "If you're innocent, then you have nothing to worry about." These were not the people you see in the movies, no one looked beautiful or even normal, they were either too skinny or too fat, they had acne, they had creepy haircuts, their lives were one long series of excuses, they were poor, even the ones who thought they had money didn't have any. How could anyone live on twenty thousand dollars a year? He guessed that he was looking at people who kept families on ten thousand. How could anyone support a family on less than fifty thousand? Who among these Americans, dressed in clothes they bought off the racks in discount drug stores and large supermarkets, could imagine a salary of five hundred or seven hundred thousand dollars a year? With free credit cards. And I know millionaires, he thought. I have talked to men worth two hundred million dollars. I've talked to men worth a billion dollars! Could any of these miserable people sitting on badly molded fiberglass chairs and staring at this linoleum floor imagine that kind of money? Did these people go to the movies? he wondered. Did they have the time or money? Or were they beyond the popular culture? Black men, Mexican women, children. Old people. What were they doing at the police station? How many of them were murderers? And of those who were, was that the only bond between them and Griffin? Yes, he thought. He would hate his cell mates.

Susan Avery came out to meet him. Was it standard for her to leave her office and greet each visitor, instead of having them sent back to her, or was she treating him well because he was important? Or was she going to walk behind him in case he smelled a trap and tried to run?

"I'm sorry I'm late," he said. "I had a few calls that had to be returned."

"Your work must be very exciting."

""It's not all movie stars and caviar, but it changes all the time. I imagine you don't have much routine."

"Paperwork," she said, holding up a finger as a gesture of exclamation, as a reminder that he should know it wasn't easy being a cop, or that without the paperwork it would be fun, would be easy.

She had an office with a window overlooking the parking lot. She closed the door. There was a poster on it of a kitten dangling from a chin-up bar, with the inscription, HANG IN THERE.

She offered him coffee. He refused. They settled down.

"So, you must have a break in the case," he said.

"What makes you say that?"

"Why else would you bring me here?"

"Did you follow David Kahane to his car?"

"No."

"Where did you park your car?"

"A block away, on the street."

"Why didn't you use the parking lot?" She really wanted to know. He had to repeat to himself, while he was thinking of the answer, that she was just curious, that he wasn't a suspect.

Hadn't they been over this already? He couldn't remember. "There was a space on the street. I don't even think I knew about the parking lot."

"There's a sign over the theater marquee that says FREE PARKING IN THE REAR."

"I didn't park in the lot."

"What were you wearing that night?"

"I went straight from work, so, I don't know . . . what I'm wearing now, I guess. A dress shirt, slacks, leather shoes."

"Jacket and tie?"

"If I wear one, I always take off my tie at the end of the day."

"And the jacket?"

"I don't remember."

"What color jacket do you think you might have been wearing? How many jackets do you have?"

"I have about thirty jackets."

She raised an eyebrow. He lifted his hands and held them apart, to tell her, "What can I say, I have my vanities." Then he said, "I can't throw anything out." He tried to sound like he was making fun of his own sissiness.

"Which one were you wearing that night?"

"I usually wear a dark jacket to work. I have a couple of plaids and a few sort of khaki-colored jackets, and a Harris Tweed and a corduroy jacket with leather elbow patches, but I usually wear black or blue." He wondered if he should say something like, Why are you asking me these questions, or whether he should say that if she asked him any more of these kinds of questions, he would demand to have a lawyer present. What kinds of questions? she would respond. Questions that you'd ask of a suspect, not a witness. But you're not a witness. That's right, I'm just someone who saw David Kahane a little while before he died.

"We wanted you to look at some pictures. You might recognize someone." She pulled a folder from a file and passed him a few mug shots. A thin man with sparse blond hair and a fixed nose, wearing a gold chain. A depressed black man. A dark-haired man with a mustache—an Iranian, probably—his hair was shiny and thick and he had a narrow face with a serious nose. He hoped he might recognize one, but he didn't. He nodded at the man with the blond hair.

"I don't know, there's something familiar about him."

"You think you saw him that night?"

"I'd never say that in court. I mean, I don't know. I don't like being put in this position where just because someone looks like maybe I've seen him before, he could get arrested or something." He hoped he was doubtful enough, that he sounded like a regular guy. He had chosen the blond man because he looked weak. Or had he picked the blond man because he had the same round face as Griffin? If there was ever a lineup, Griffin would choose the one who looked most like him. If there had been a witness, then Griffin would have to corroborate his description. He knew that the police usually threw in ringers among these pictures, or at least they did in lineups, using innocent men, other cops, to make sure that the sample was mixed. Obviously someone who had seen the murder from a distance had come forward, but this witness's description was tentative. Not tentative, no, the description sounded like Griffin. And now Susan Avery was trying to understand why or how Griffin might have killed David Kahane. How could they prove me guilty of a senseless murder? he wondered. Could they?

She took the photographs back. He thought about asking her out for a date. "Are these real suspects?"

"What do you mean by real?"

"Motive and opportunity."

"A lot of killers have strange motives."

"This was a robbery, right?"

"If that was the motive, then all we need is to show opportunity. Even you had opportunity."

What would the innocent person say? "Please," he said, "that's a very unpleasant thought. I'd hate to think that all that separates anyone from murder is lack of opportunity. I guess you see the dark side a lot more than I do, but I try to believe that people are basically good." He had tried to make her believe that when she had pointed the finger at him, she meant it to be an absurd notion, an example of her worldview, not a real accusation.

"I thought Hollywood was a sea of sharks."

"First of all, sharks live by instinct, and I don't think it's fair to say that because of that they're basically evil. Second of all, yes, there are some really awful people in the business, and you don't always know who you can trust. But you don't have to be a bad guy. There are also a lot of people in the business who are decent, who are honest, who you can trust. Me, I'm in the middle." He smiled. Susan Avery looked confused.

"You mean it."

"Oh, yeah. Absolutely. I'm not completely trustworthy. I'd be lying if I said I was. Well, personally, with friends, I guess I'm okay, but the office, the job, demands a certain amount of game playing. Only it's real life, so the game can hurt." He stopped. How good a cop is she? he thought. She was fascinated. He could tell her that if honesty is a weapon, then it's not honesty, not if you use it as a tool. He could, but he wouldn't. "How did we get on to this, Doctor? And should I start telling you about my childhood?"

"Go ahead." She was flirting with him.

He wagged a finger. "Uh-uh. That would have to be after hours."

"I don't think my boyfriend would go for that." Why was he down here? he wanted to ask. Was it really only about the mug shots? Was she coming on to him?

"Is he also a cop?"

"He's a contractor."

"Been together long?"

"A year. Do you have anyone?"

"A few." He didn't want to continue this conversation. He was disappointed with her, she hadn't seen through him, he wasn't a suspect, he wasn't under arrest. Maybe there really was a witness, but Avery had looked forward to seeing him, Griffin thought, and she had wasted his time.

"Do you go out with actresses?" What kind of question was that?

"Lieutenant, Detective, Miss Avery . . . Susan . . ." It was time for him to assert all of his rank. "I'd love to help you find the person who killed David Kahane. I'm sorry he died, but I barely knew him, so I can afford the luxury of being fascinated by the whole process of how you go about your work. Who knows what I'll learn from this, what I might be able to add to a movie from all of this, you know, I mean, I don't think I've ever been this deep into a police station, it's nice to have an authentic experience. But I don't have time, this afternoon, to talk about . . ."—he had to lighten up—". . . my very sad love life."

"When would you have time?"

"I'll call you."

They shook hands. She offered to show him to the front, and he refused. He wouldn't call her. On the chance that she did, after all, think he had killed David Kahane, he didn't want to let her try to trip him up. And he was worried that he might give himself away. What if they went to bed together and he talked in his sleep? Bed? Would she sleep with him to get a conviction?

CHAPTER TWELVE

Oakley and Civella were waiting in his office when he came back from the police station. He was fifteen minutes late. Civella was on the phone, yelling at one of his clients, a singer. Civella didn't like a song he wanted to put on his next album.

"We'll talk about this later," he said, watching Griffin, and he hung up. "Griffin, what was I in my last life that I deserve to manage songwriters? What was I? Was I that much of a monster? All the talent in the world and no taste."

"Talking about youself again, are you?" said Tom Oakley.

"The English are the meanest people in the world," said Civella. "Just on a simple human conversational level, they're the meanest."

Griffin didn't want the banter to continue. "Have you worked out the story?"

Civella pressed back into his chair. "When we tell you the story, are you prepared to commit within eighteen hours?"

Griffin understood that he was being challenged to make the deal before they took the story someplace else. "Why not twenty-four?"

"Because that would give you until five o'clock tomorrow, and I don't want to lose a full day. I have meetings scheduled at two other studios. We think it's good, we think we can set it up, if not here, you know we can get a deal with someone else, and you did tell us not to pitch it anywhere else. In consideration of which, we want the answer within eighteen hours."

"What if it took me three days to say yes?"

"Then you'd lose it."

"And if you were turned down everywhere else? And I still wanted it? Then I could tell Business Affairs to see how hungry you were."

"You just saw me yelling at someone who made five million dollars last year, and I get twenty percent, and he's not my biggest client."

"But you've never produced a movie. So it doesn't really matter how much money you've made. You want this and you're hungry."

"I've produced three movies."

"You put the sound tracks together for three movies and you got to call yourself an Executive Producer. I won't hold that against you. I told you I liked this idea when I heard it in the Polo Lounge, and I haven't heard anything yet to change my mind. And yes, I'll let you know by eleven tomorrow."

Griffin knew he was going to say yes. He wanted to pass this project off to Larry Levy. Civella and Oakley, who was silent, and probably depressed, mad at his producer for putting at risk a deal he needed, not just for the movie but for the money, would never be able to pull off *Habeas Corpus*, but it sounded good. Someone would bite. Death row, a beautiful woman on the stand for her life, a D.A. with a mission, the capital punishment debate against the background of a steamy murder, the project sounded like it was sure to attract movie stars. It may have been their idea, but Civella and Oakley were the wrong people for this story, which needed someone who had proven his skill with difficult material. If Levy could be persuaded that *Habeas Corpus* was the next movie in the line of *Body Heat, Jagged Edge,* and *Fatal Attraction,* he would want it for himself, but Levy could never stand up to Civella, and Civella would hate Levy. Civella would tell Levy how the story should go, and Civella would never be able to wring the best story out of Oakley, who looked too tired for the job.

"I want to introduce you to someone," said Griffin. "Larry Levy, he's new here, do you know him?"

"I've met him a couple of times," said Civella. Oakley knew the name.

Griffin asked Jan to get Larry for him. She came back in ten seconds. "He's not here. He just left for a doctor's appointment." Griffin wondered if that would be his analyst.

"So he's in his car. Perfect. Do you have the number?"

"I'll connect," she said.

Griffin turned on the speakerphone. Jan came on. "I got him."

Levy said, "Hello?"

"Hello, Larry," said Griffin. "Do you have a few minutes?"

"About ten. I've got a meeting at CAA, I'm on my way there."

So it is his shrink. Griffin was glad that Levy was lying. Oakley and Civella hadn't heard he was supposed to be going to a doctor. "Larry, I'd like you to hear an idea. I've got Andy Civella and Tom Oakley with me. It's a good idea."

"Welcome to the modern world," said Levy. "And of course you've got me on the speakerphone too?"

"Yes, Larry, you are."

"Hello, Larry, this is Andy Civella."

"And this is Tom Oakley."

"What's new?"

Oakley knew how to pitch. If he'd been selling a cathedral, he wouldn't have talked about size or height, he would have quickly run through the dimensions and then, as though assuming that the cardinal to whom he was speaking knew that dimension was the ace card that all the other, the ordinary architects would play, he would dispense with measurement, take a deep breath, and say, "But it's really about the doors." Then he'd talk about light, and what you see when you first enter, throw in a few descriptions of the rose windows, maybe describe the nave, and where he'd put the baptismal fonts, and then sit down. Oakley, whose depression lifted as he talked, did not mind that he was telling his story to a speakerphone on a desk. He understood that this was business, and in business you save your energy for the deal, for closing the deal. Griffin wondered if this small sign of dignity meant that Oakley would get along with Levy and turn in a script that Levison would make. In that case Griffin would have been handing a gun to Levy with permission to shoot him. Oakley told a good story about a man who believed in justice but who now feels that there's a flaw in the notion of justice, unless even the rich get the chair. He told a good story about a bad marriage, and when he came to the husband's missing corpse, Levy interrupted him and said he felt a chill. He shouldn't have said anything, thought Griffin. It would be harder to negotiate with Civella if he knew the studio really wanted the project. Oakley skipped to the end of the story and cut between the woman in the gas chamber and the man forcing his way into the prison to save her life.

Civella smiled proudly at Griffin while Oakley plunged ahead. Of course, the story still hadn't been worked out, and the architect was still pointing to the windows instead of the supports that would hold up the walls that would contain the windows. The cardinal was hooked, though. Only later would he find out that the flying buttress needed to be invented, and if the windows were finally blessed, that service would be performed by another cardinal, in another lifetime. Oakley's story still lacked a flying buttress. But the windows were pretty.

"Griffin, take me off the speakerphone." Civella patted Oakley's hand. Griffin wanted that touch for himself. He picked up the receiver.

"What time are you coming back?" he asked Levy.

"About six o'clock. How late are you staying?"

"I'll be around."

"Has anyone else heard this?"

"No."

"It's good. You know it's good."

"Mmm-hmm."

"We should make a deal now. Tomorrow will be too late. It's guaranteed they've got other meetings on this."

"Mmm-hmm."

"I'll see you when I come back."

"If I need to call you, who are you seeing?"

"What?"

"At CAA?"

"You won't need to call me."

Griffin hung up the phone. Levy thought he was playing hardball by refusing to answer. Pathetic.

"Well," said Civella, "he said yes."

"Don't open the champagne until you hear from me."

"By tomorrow morning?"

"That's what I promised."

"I don't understand," said Oakley. "Do we have a deal?"

"Yes," said the manager. The three of them walked slowly to the door.

"Not yet," said Griffin. "But it looks good."

Griffin watched as Civella and Oakley passed Jan's desk without looking at her. They went into the hall and stopped at a photograph of Glenn Ford in a Western. Oakley tapped it with his knuckles—for luck, Griffin supposed. Civella wrapped an arm around Oakley's shoulders and gave him a wonderful, friendly hug. Griffin heard Civella say, "You did good. That was a very difficult situation. You did just great." Then they were gone.

"You said yes, huh?" asked Jan.

"Probably."

"Good idea?"

"I think so. It is a good idea. It is."

"Buyer's remorse?"

"Maybe a little." He was telling her the truth. He felt the way he did whenever he bought something to wear. Was this the right choice? He wasn't even thinking about Larry Levy, or the Writer, or the Pasadena police. There was comfort in this. He was having a natural reaction. Anyone in his position would feel some trepidation over committing to a new project, even people who hadn't killed. He went back into his office.

Bonnie Sherow called from New York. "Griffin, I'm sorry. I know we're supposed to go to the Motion Picture Home thing tonight, but I couldn't get out of here. I thought I was going to get a ride on the company jet, but there wasn't room."

"Did you get the book?"

"We'll know tomorrow."

"That's all that matters."

"But this dinner. You know, I wanted to see you."

"Business before pleasure." He wasn't sure why he said that.

"I know, I know." She believed it. She tried to live it.

"Where are you staying?"

"Essex House. Why?"

"Don't ask."

"See you in a few days."

"Absolutely."

She hung up. First he called a florist, who promised immediate delivery of a seventy-dollar arrangement to Bonnie's room in New York. It was after seven there, and he had to pay a thirty-dollar premium. A hundred dollars. He charged it to the studio.

Then he called June Mercator, to invite her to the ball.

"When is it?" she asked.

"Tonight. Eight o'clock."

"But that's in three hours."

"I know, I know."

"Your first choice canceled."

"She's in New York."

"Will you tell her you took me?"

"She'll find out."

"This is one of these things where the company buys a table and we'll sit with all the people you work with?"

"Something like that."

"How will you introduce me?"

"I'll say, 'This is June Mercator.'"

"You'll pick me up?"

She gave him her address. She lived in the Hollywood Hills, on Outpost. The address was familiar, the same block as Levison's old house, before Levison moved to Brentwood. There were beautiful houses up there, with backyards and views of the city. They cost half a million dollars, at least. Again he wondered how Kahane afforded his life. Kahane was lucky to have had this woman, to have known her. It would be easy to say she was cool, but she was better than that. She was calm. Was she still in mourning? Had she really mourned Kahane? Had Griffin relieved her of the hard job of breaking up? Had she hated Kahane, and did she now love Griffin for all the things lacking in her old lover? The house must be hers, Griffin thought. If it was Kahane's, wouldn't she be worrying about where to live next? They weren't married, after all, so the house would go to his family, unless he'd left a will. Would he have left a will? I should make a will, thought Griffin. I own my own house and I don't have a will. Maybe they owned it together. Maybe it belongs to her.

Larry Levy came back from his doctor's appointment. He called Griffin into his office.

"Can Oakley do it?" he asked.

"I think so," said Griffin.

"Have you ever worked with him?"

"No."

"I checked him out. He's supposed to be okay."

"Good. I'll tell Levison."

"We'll tell him together."

Levison was on the phone when Celia let them pass into his office. It sounded like he was talking to his wife. When he finished, he looked to Levy for the meeting's reason.

"Griffin had me listen to a pitch from Tom Oakley and Andy Civella." Good, thought Griffin. He's already assuming responsibility for this one.

"Not Tom Oakley," said Levison. "He had some real promise for a while, but he's turning into a hack."

"I figured you might say that, but I think the idea is pretty good, and that's why I asked Larry to hear it."

"It's good," said Levy. "It's real good."

"Tell me," said Levison.

"Dustin Hoffman sends Kathleen Turner to the gas chamber, but when he finds out she's innocent, he has to break into the prison to save her life." Levy was sharper than Oakley, thought Griffin; he had the pitch down to twenty-five words.

Levison was quiet for almost a minute. "Do they fuck?"

"We'll get there," said Levy.

"And Tom Oakley wants to write this? What's it called?"

"*Habeas Corpus,*" said Griffin.

"Will he be expensive?"

"He thinks he will," said Levy, "but we'll make him humble."

"A hundred for the first draft, including two sets of revisions."

"Against what?" asked Griffin.

"Against whatever. Two-fifty, three-fifty. And, Larry, I think you should work with them on it. Is that okay with you, Griffin? Will they mind?"

"I don't know. They might."

"Make the deal first."

"Fine," said Griffin. "Just let me tell them the good news."

On their way back down the hall, Levy told Griffin he felt awkward getting a project that started with him.

"No," said Griffin, "don't worry about it. If the movie works, we'll all look good."

It was six-thirty. He called the Beverly Hills Hotel. Civella was out. He started to leave the one-word message, "Yes," but stopped. This was not the time to be cute. "Just tell him to check in with Griffin Mill." He might send champagne to be gracious. Oakley would be happy, and probably a little scared of the responsibility. Civella would be triumphant. Griffin wished he could join their celebration.

It was time to pick up June Mercator. His black tie was in the closet. There was a shower in a washroom down the hall. He took extra care to shave closely. He loved wearing the black tie, though he wouldn't admit this to anyone, but maybe that was how everyone felt. He knew he looked good.

CHAPTER THIRTEEN

Perhaps we'll get married and have children, Griffin thought. If there is a son, will June want to name him David? Griffin decided that if there was a boy, that was the name he would suggest. Maybe not. If he called him David, would he ever look at him without thinking about the parking lot and the smell of the air escaping from the tire? Or would calling him David bring out a kind of tenderness? Because I took a life, I have now made a life. David. Good morning, David. How was school today, David? Let's play catch, David. Why don't you ask your friends to come to Aspen with us for Christmas, David? David, I think you're in love. David, it's time we had a talk. David, I'm not without guilt. June might say that name belongs to the past. This was assuming that she loved David Kahane the night he died.

It was a little after seven. He had ordered a limousine, and the driver was waiting for him at the door. There were nights when everyone took a limousine, and this was one of them. Griffin wasn't sure that he wanted June to see him arrive in a long Cadillac; he wanted her to think of him as a regular guy for someone so important, but he measured that against how it would look to drive up to the Hilton in his own car while his opposite numbers from other studios stepped out of limousines. Would she really think that he was just one of the guys if he picked her up in his Mercedes?

The house was almost at the top of Outpost. It was set back from the street and up a small rise. The garden in front was well tended, like an old country club, or a mission-style church, a few palms, some large-leafed jungle plants, and a freshly cut lawn. The house was Spanish, with a heavy oak door and a stained-glass insert, shaped like a diamond, behind a wrought-iron grill. It was nicer than his house, he thought, more refined, better built, the kind of place people with character live in, people who know artists. He felt ashamed for all the new fixtures in his house, the expensive bathroom, the kitchen cabinets that closed so quietly. Would June approve?

The black Saab was in the driveway, the glue from the dealer's sticker still in the window.

When the door opened, June started to say hello, but he watched her stop for a second as she looked over his shoulder to the limousine at the curb and the driver standing beside it. She shook Griffin's hand and led him inside. She wore a pretty gown that combined midnight blue and a bit of black.

"You look great," said Griffin.

"Come inside."

"We're sort of in a rush."

"Just let me get off the phone." She walked quickly back to the kitchen. She was arguing with a printer about a late order. "The bank is very unhappy," she said. "Do you understand? The bank is very unhappy. It's Wednesday or never, Ben. Deliver the brochures by Wednesday or throw them out. It's up to you."

She came out of the kitchen, her eyes bright.

"Sounds like you were having fun," said Griffin.

"Actually we have two weeks before we need the brochures, and Ben knows that, but he's slow. Anyway, would you like a glass of wine? No, of course not, we have to go."

"Beautiful house."

"It was either clean it up or find something to wear. I'll give you the tour another time."

As they walked to the car, Griffin realized that if he slept with her in the house, he'd probably make love in David Kahane's bed. If he needed to brush his teeth, he'd be given Kahane's toothbrush. Well, not his actual toothbrush—she would have thrown it out—but unless she bought new brushes after his death, any brushes hidden in a drawer might have been chosen by the man he murdered. This was the most gruesome thought he'd had since the night in the parking lot.

June accepted the limousine driver's official servant's nod as she got into the car. She took her seat in the limousine and started talking to Griffin as though this happened to her every day, to be called to a charity ball with three hours' notice and to be driven there by a chauffeur. Griffin wanted to make a joke about the car, but he couldn't think of something that wouldn't make fun of the luxury. He didn't know whether it would be more amusing to act as though he was used to it or that it was new to him. He said nothing.

"Tell me about yourself," she said.

"What would you like to know?"

"The usual."

"Where I went to high school, what my major is, what dorm I live in, that sort of stuff?"

"Yes." She really wanted to know, and she didn't want to make a joke about it. The impatience carried by her tone of voice started a faster pace in Griffin's pulse. It scared him.

"I'm from Michigan. Lansing. Have you ever met anyone from Lansing?"

"I don't think so."

"You haven't, I know. I've never met anyone else from Lansing, Michigan, either. Anyway, my father was a judge, my mother was head of the board of education. She died three years ago. He's retired and lives in Georgia, on the coast. I went to the University of Michigan. I was an art major."

"An *art* major." She put the emphasis on *art;* everyone was always surprised when they found that out.

"What's the surprise, that a studio executive was an art major, or that I was, I mean, the person you see in front of you, this bland-looking kind of square guy. Can't picture him worried about paint?"

"Is that how I sounded?"

"It's all right. I'm used to it. I really was a painter. I was very good, actually, by the standards of the art department. It was sort of like cooking; I knew the recipe. I knew how to get the faculty jury to give me the prizes. Then I figured out how to get on the jury, to get on all the right committees. I always got along great with adults. I went to New York after

Michigan, graduate school at NYU, and I was friendlier with film-school people than painters, and I dropped out of the painting program. Then I spent a few months in the film school and got friendly with the faculty, and one day the head of a big agency came to lecture, and I had to pick him up at the airport. I left for Los Angeles with him the next day. He put me in the mail room. I worked there for two months, I read every script I could. I decided I didn't want to be an agent, I got a job as a reader, and one thing led to another and here I am. I've always been lucky about being in the right place."

"Do you still paint?"

"Sometimes. I was okay. I wasn't fooling anyone. I also knew that I wasn't great. I was a good academic painter. But I was stuck in abstract expressionism. When the conceptualists came long, I was dead. I would have made an excellent teacher, but things went a different way. It's not this big from-Art-to-Hollywood story. It didn't work like that."

"You sound a little defensive."

"It's an easy thing for people to pick on."

"Who?"

"The people who pick on Hollywood for being artless. The people who still believe in capital-A Art."

"Now you sound cynical."

"No, now I'm being defensive." It was fun talking in a limousine. You could look at each other. It was like a party.

There were other limousines on Santa Monica Boulevard, a long line of them turning right to the Hilton. The great moment of the limousine is the arrival. June reached overhead to a makeup light and took a compact from her purse. How did she know the light was there? She finished putting on her makeup and then smiled at Griffin. The smile was forced. Hadn't she taken a limousine to Kahane's burial? That's where she learned about the makeup light. No. The Saab was at the funeral home. Someone else had driven the Saab. She looked away from Griffin and held the compact in her hand. He thought by the way she held it, measuring the weight, that it might have been a gift from Kahane, although he didn't think it looked like a gift, it was just a department-store compact. It was a brief glimpse into the sadness she still felt at David Kahane's death. The limousine was at the entrance. Someone was opening her door.

"Look," she said, "there's Robin Williams."

The driver opened Griffin's door. He had something to say.

"We were followed. From the time we left the studio. I wasn't sure until we picked up your friend, but the car that followed us drove past her house on Outpost, and then, when we started back down the hill, he was after us again. It pulled into the public parking lot as we pulled in here. A Dodge Charger."

"Did you see the driver?"

"I think so. Some guy with short hair and a mustache."

"Thanks."

"See you later."

June waited for Griffin on the sidewalk. He came around the back of the limousine and took her arm and brought her to the center of the red carpet, where Robin Williams faced a half dozen photographers. He pretended to be Mighty Joe Young in chains, in the nightclub scene where he comes out of the pit while Terry Moore plays "Beautiful Dreamer" on the piano. Then he turned into King Kong frightened by flashbulbs and driven insane. He started to make Terry Moore into Nancy Reagan. Griffin called out to him, "Robin!"

The actor smiled. "Hello, Mr. Thalberg," he said. Someone took their picture together.

Griffin introduced him to June. She seemed polite, not too star-struck, but not diffident, either. She seemed more impressed with Griffin for knowing Robin Williams than for actually shaking the actor's hand.

There was no one with short hair and a mustache hanging around the edge of the crowd. As they followed the red carpet to the ballroom, Griffin wondered how he looked to June. He was aware of himself the way he might be aware of his house if he walked a prospective buyer through it, noticing all the details he'd taken for granted. Did he really know so many people as he was greeting? There were fifteen hundred people in the room, and he knew their faces the way a popular senior knows his class in high school. When they greeted him, they studied June Mercator, though only for a second. Griffin didn't make an effort to introduce her, so she didn't register. How did he look to the man with short hair?

"Why did he call you Mr. Thalberg?" asked June.

"Irving Thalberg was the boy wonder of 1933. He was Louis B. Mayer's head of production."

"They give that award at the Oscars. What's it for?"

"Contributions to the industry. I'm not up for it." She laughed at this in a way that suggested friendship, how a friend would tease someone without drawing blood, the issue here was professional self-respect, not an area Griffin dwelt upon too often, but it was the kind of question he could imagine worrying about when he was old—what was his life worth?—and June's laugh said she forgave him. So she was starting to like him. When he'd called David Kahane and June answered the phone, she had been impressed with him, not that he'd done anything, just the fact that he'd called, that it was really Griffin Mill on the line. Since then, even through her brief period of mourning, she'd watched him, tested him. Now he knew she was ready to have fun with him, she was ready for a thrill. He wanted to tell her it wasn't him, it was the limousine, it was Robin Williams. No, he thought, what else am I but these little pieces?

The studio's table was close to the stage. Levison was there with his wife, Andrea. Her father had been on the board of MGM in the old days, and she knew three generations of everyone. She worked for a few charities, but tonight's wasn't one of them. She'd started a mail-order business with two other wives, but nothing had come of it. Sometimes he thought she seemed trapped inside herself, or someone did, someone who hated her husband and hated California, someone who would be happier selling hooked rugs in Vermont. Griffin always asked about the children, and she was always glad to answer him. They liked each other. She understood the politics of the office, and so there was always this awareness between them; that was all there had to be to kill the possible friendship, just an awareness of the office. Griffin introduced June to the Levisons, and then to the others at the table. Andrea greeted June with glazed good manners, never expecting to see her again. There was no reason for Andrea to know that Griffin had been talking to Bonnie Sherow again, although Andrea had liked her and, after their breakup, asked after her a few times.

Levison had also invited the head of the legal department and his wife, and a few people from Business Affairs, the television division, and his doctor, a serious and quiet man who ran marathons.

It was the doctor who found the postcard, under his dinner plate. "Look at this," he said, holding up a picture of a naked Polynesian woman standing in a Tahitian waterfall.

"Did we all get one?" asked Andrea. Everyone looked under their plates. Griffin couldn't see if there was anything written on the back. He waited for someone to ask if there was a message.

"Maybe it's part of a door-prize drawing," said one of the Business Affairs people.

"How so?" asked Greene.

"Maybe the person who finds it gets a trip to Tahiti."

"No," said the head of the legal department. "They wouldn't just hand out a trip by sticking it at the table of a big studio. It's just a busboy's idea of a practical joke."

"Does it say anything?" asked June. Griffin felt that he had willed her to ask this.

"No," said Greene.

No one at the table thought the mystery of the card was worth pursuing, and the doctor slipped it next to the floral centerpiece. Would normal curiosity allow Griffin to ask to see the card? The card was a long reach over June's section of the table. If she left for the bathroom, he could get it easily. He'd wait. No, he decided, since there was no message, he should ignore it.

Dessert was over. The house lights dimmed. Joan Rivers was at the podium. Griffin excused himself from the table. June squeezed his hand as he got up. He patted her shoulder. If he asked her to marry him tonight, fly to Las Vegas and do it in an all-night wedding chapel, she'd probably say yes.

He walked around the edge of the ballroom as the crowd laughed. The smell of perfume, makeup, shoe polish, food, a few cigarettes, the waves of laughter, the overwhelming mood of satisfaction and the tincture of panic within that happiness, from those who were worried about their jobs, or about their next project, this flood of sensations was suddenly overwhelmingly poignant to Griffin, sunset over Rome from a hotel window. This is my life, he wanted to tell them all. You are my people, I am one of you. This party is not just a thing I have to do. I am happy here.

An usher held a curtain aside for him, and he went through a door into the lobby, to find a man with short hair and a mustache. The photographers waited outside the hotel's entrance. Griffin walked through the lobby toward the coffee shop, around a corner. In the coffee shop he bought a Milky Way bar and tore off the wrapper while the woman at the cash register made his change. Then he walked outside to Wilshire Boulevard. Here he was, in a tuxedo, eating chocolate in Beverly Hills. He walked west on Wilshire, around the hotel's offices, then back to the front entrance. No one was following him.

Inside the lobby again, he went to the elevators. He saw the short-haired man as he passed the entrance to the ballroom. He was about thirty-five, Griffin thought, and he couldn't remember the face at all. He was well groomed, his hair was cut short, with slightly long sideburns. His face was weathered. How could a writer get so much sun? He wore dark gray slacks and a blue blazer with a brown tie. Griffin didn't remember him at all. This nonrecognition came with a tide of regret. How often does this happen? thought Griffin, feeling sorry for the Writer. How many people do I meet who don't register? If I was as frustrated as this man, would I have sent those silly postcards? Would I have killed?

He'd been gone from the table for almost ten minutes. It was a long time, but it couldn't be helped. He could go back into the ballroom, but he thought that if this was a movie, then it was time to confront the dragon. He wanted the third act now.

He turned away from the ballroom and headed to the elevators. The short-haired man stayed behind him. Griffin nodded to him, and the man joined him in an elevator going up. A bellboy with a cart stacked with luggage waited until they were inside and then joined them.

The bellboy asked Griffin for his floor.

"Five," said Griffin. The bellboy touched the button for him. Then the bellboy got off on three. As soon as the doors closed behind him, Griffin turned to face the short-haired man.

"You have to understand, it's a very difficult job. I see people all day long. My phone rings a hundred times a day. Take all the stories that are presented to the studio, either in pitches, as scripts, or as books and magazine articles that get covered, and we are talking about seventy thousand stories in a year."

The door opened. Griffin got out. The short-haired man stayed with him, watching him. The hallway was quiet.

"I don't know how I can make it up to you. I'm sorry that I hurt people's feelings along the way. I'm trying to be better, I really am. But you're going too far. It's an incredibly difficult business. You can have great ideas, you can have all the talent in the world, but you have to get lucky. And no one has the formula for luck. The only consolation to this is that once you get lucky, you look different, and then it gets easier."

Griffin watched for a response. The man stared at him. Griffin pushed for the elevator, pressing both the up and down buttons. He wanted to get away.

"I have to get back to the party. Maybe you should come in again and tell me a story. Tell me everything you've got. Usually we only like to hear one at a time, but obviously you've got an active imagination; maybe we can channel all that anger to something good." Griffin tried to get the man to smile. He didn't.

"You're not going to kill me, are you?" asked Griffin.

"No. Why should I kill you?"

"Who are you?"

"I'm not who you think I am."

An elevator going up stopped at the floor. Griffin got in, the man followed. They rode to the top floor and back to the lobby.

If this man was the postcard Writer, then either Griffin had a terrible memory or this man was a blank who made no impression on anyone and walked the earth indignant. If this man was not the postcard Writer, then either he was the man the limousine driver had seen following them or he was not that man, he was just a person in the hotel. But if he was just a person in the hotel, then why did he ride the elevator with Griffin? Was he homosexual, had he interpreted Griffin's stroll around the hotel as a cruise? If this man had not followed him all night, then either the limousine driver was mistaken and no one had followed them, or the person in the Dodge Charger was the postcard Writer and he was elsewhere in the hotel. Dressed as a waiter? How else could he have found Griffin's table? There was another possibility. That this man was not the person in the Dodge Charger, and the driver of the Charger, though he was somewhere else, was also not the postcard Writer. Or this man drove the Dodge Charger but was not the Writer.

Griffin didn't know if he should be scared of this man or embarrassed that he'd just given a speech that sounded insane to someone who didn't care. If the man was homosexual, then by now he knew that following Griffin had been a mistake, and was he scared of him? If this man wasn't the Writer, then where was he? Who was in the Dodge Charger?

When they left the elevator, the man turned toward the lobby as Griffin headed toward the ballroom. Before he went in, he looked back to see if the man was still there. He was at a display of tour brochures next to the bell captain's desk.

Griffin showed his pass and walked into the ballroom, where Neil Diamond was on the stage, and the crowd was clapping in time to the song. Someone—Griffin couldn't see who—put out a hand to greet him as he passed a table in the dark. He touched it lightly and moved ahead to find his own table, and June Mercator.

She sat sideways in her chair. Griffin was surprised to see her clapping; he wouldn't have thought she liked such a sentimental entertainer, but Neil Diamond was a strong performer, and he was only twenty feet away.

Griffin touched her shoulder as he took his seat. "Having fun?"

"Don't tell anyone you saw me singing along with Neil Diamond."

He kissed her behind the ear, moving her hair aside to touch her neck. She leaned into the kiss, and he took a little breath, not so much to inhale her perfume as to rest for a moment.

"Where were you?" she asked.

"I wasn't feeling well."

"Oh, I'm sorry. Why didn't you say something? Is it your stomach?"

"I was just feeling a little claustropobic. I needed some air. I took a walk."

"You okay now?"

"Fine."

"Poor baby." She kissed him on the cheek, with a disappointing lack of pressure. Her lips were dry, it was halfway between a mommy kissing the cut and an old girlfriend giving a kiss for consolation after he'd come to her with the story of a disastrous affair. Her familiarity, which he thought at first signaled the understanding that they'd end up in bed, now promised a passionless friendship. She'd confide in him, but he'd never see her naked. He wanted to see her without her clothes. She needed to be convinced. She needed persuasion. He would negotiate with a few gestures. When she looked back at the singer, he kissed her just above the spot where her neck and collarbone met. She drifted a little, toward him. He put his hand between her chair and the small of her back, and he rubbed her waist. He thought she might hate this because he could grab an inch of fat, but if he stopped, then she'd think he was upset by the extra weight, and how much was it, ten pounds? More. He pushed his hand toward her stomach and then touched the bottom of her breast before letting go. He kissed her on the cheek, and then on the ear. She lowered her head a little, tilted it forward, offering her neck once again. It was another gesture from her grief.

Levison was watching him. Griffin smiled at him, trying to look shy and proud. Levison grinned back, his lips pursed, and he nodded his approval of June, or of Griffin's luck. Neil Diamond finished his song. Fifteen hundred people stood and cheered.

Two women, one the wife of the head of an agency, the other the wife of the owner of a studio, came out onstage and presented the singer with an award for his contributions to the Motion Picture Home. Then they asked for the lights to be dimmed once again, and a movie screen descended and they introduced a film about the Home. June turned back in her chair and finished the wine remaining in her glass.

"Do you want to stay?" asked Griffin.

"You have to, don't you?"

"I don't think so. Let's go." Griffin left his seat and walked around the table to Levison. He told him he was going.

"I shouldn't leave yet," said Levison. "I'll see you tomorrow."

June shook hands with Levison and his wife and said good-bye to the doctor. Griffin took her arm as they walked through the maze of tables, and after they had separated for a moment, she took his hand.

The short-haired man was gone from the lobby. Outside, the limousine drivers stood by their cars and smoked. Griffin's driver left a circle of five men and disappeared into the garage to get the car.

"That was fun," said June.

"Did you want to stay?"

"You've been to hundreds of these things. They must all be the same."

If he told her he loved them, what would she think?

"I love them."

"I guess you'd have to; otherwise; how could you stay in the business?"

"It's all part of the game."

Their limousine was at the curb. The driver came around and opened June's door. After she got in, he took Griffin around the back of the car.

"I didn't have anything better to do, so I found the Dodge Charger. There were some papers on the backseat. It looks like we were followed by someone from the Pasadena Police."

"Maybe he was following you," said Griffin. His heart wanted to stop. What had he said to the man in the elevator? Had he confessed?

"I haven't been to Pasadena in four months, since the Rose Bowl."

"I don't know when I was there. Maybe two years ago."

"Maybe they're after your friend."

"Should we tell her?" asked Griffin. He thought this was his master-stroke question, it screamed his innocence.

"That's up to you."

"Hey, this is a first date. Let sleeping dogs lie, you know what I mean?"

He winked, and as the driver opened Griffin's door, he winked back. If he was expecting a larger tip, as hush money, Griffin wouldn't pay it. Better to look unconcerned. After all, the problem was the woman's, not his.

He sat down beside June; their legs touched as the car changed lanes.

"That was fun," she said. The limousine entered the flow of cars on Wilshire. Other drivers and passengers tried to look through the tinted windows, but it was Griffin and June, invisible to them, who were the voyeurs. There was always a feeling of warm entitlement that came with riding in a limousine. Griffin was used to it; it was impossible to feel a kinship with ordinary people in dented, rusted cars with uncomfortable seats. If he lost the job, perhaps this would be the privilege hardest to give up. Yes, and he envied the really wealthy, who had private limousines, for whom the privilege was not an illusion, who had private jet planes and private helicopters. Is this privilege an illusion? They can take it away. But is it an illusion now? If they can take it away, then it's not really mine, so yes. And June? If she was going to sleep with him tonight, and there was no reason she wouldn't, if she was enchanted with him, then wasn't she under the spell of the illusion? He was making himself sick with dizziness. This kind of thinking was beginning to hurt him. These spiraling questions! Perhaps if the limousine was his, and a helicopter and a jet plane were his, then he would finally be without illusions; he would see clearly into the true nature of things, into the reality of power.

They came to a red light, and the driver caught Griffin's attention in the rearview mirror. The Dodge Charger was beside them. The man from the elevator looked into the limousine. If he was tailing them, why had he come so close, or was he so stupid to think that the windows were dark on both sides?

The light turned green and the limousine started, but then the engine died and they stopped. The Charger, forced ahead by the traffic, continued on through the intersection.

"Sorry," said the driver. He started again, made a left turn, and the Charger was lost in the traffic ahead. In the mirror he winked at Griffin. The incident happened too quickly for June to notice.

"Where to?" asked Griffin. "Do you have to be at work early?"

Her shrug had a grain of guilt in it. "I can get away with anything for two months, maybe even a year." He understood the shrug to mean that she was closer to the end of her grief than she might let on at work. She was taking advantage of sympathy.

The cop in the Charger was making a decision now, Griffin knew. He had to choose either her place or Griffin's. If he went to Griffin's, would he call the Los Angeles Police, have them drive past June's? Maybe he would just go home to Pasadena. Hadn't he collected the most important piece of information, that the suspect and the lover were riding in a limousine just weeks after the murder? No one would doubt that they were sleeping together. How would it look to a jury? It would look bad.

And what had Griffin revealed to the man in the elevator? Fear of someone. Persecution. How would that connect with the murder of a writer in Pasadena? A conspiracy. But the police would have to ask themselves why Griffin had said so much to a stranger. How could Griffin be in a conspiracy with someone he didn't recognize? Was he being blackmailed? They would have to say Yes. And wasn't that the truth? That was the wrong question to ask of himself. He had said too much. Anything was too much. It was ridiculous for him to have imagined that he could lie to everyone.

Griffin kissed June on the cheek, with conviction. Then he kissed her on the lips. Then he sat back.

"I had to do that," he said, as though apologizing, but he was smiling. "Something came over me. I don't know what it was." If he had any lines with women, this was his favorite. It helped to play shy later in the evening, as though his official business personality, once unwound, revealed the charming little boy he once must have been.

"It was about time."

"So?"

"Would you mind coming back to my house?" she asked.

"No problem." They kissed again. Griffin didn't like making love in limousines—he'd done that enough when he was new to power and doing cocaine. Now he was embarrassed even to kiss with a driver watching. He resented June's eager kisses, he wanted her to be cooler, more discrete. He slipped away from the kiss without letting her know he was unhappy, patted her thigh, and let himself sit back in the seat so he could look at her. They held hands and didn't talk as the limousine drove along Sunset and back up to the hills. This was another of the pleasures of a limousine: contemplation.

There was no sign of the Charger near her house. Griffin signed for the limousine and then gave the driver thirty dollars. The tip was included, but Griffin decided to act the part of the happy big spender.

The driver asked if he wanted a receipt. Griffin said no. The driver thanked him.

As they walked up the path to the house, his arm around her waist, he sensed a new mood in her; she was walking slowly, trying to say something. She opened the door while he kissed the back of her neck and leaned into her body.

Inside the house, she asked him if he wanted something to drink. She went to the kitchen for mineral water. When she came back, she looked like she'd found the words for the thought she'd had on the path.

"I can't sleep with you tonight." she said. "Not here. I hope you understand."

"Actually I was wondering about that myself."

"Really?"

"I was feeling a little weird."

"Why?"

144

"I'd be the first person to make love to you since David died, right?"

"Yes."

"That's a powerful—I don't want to say 'responsibility,' I don't know— that's a charged event. I was wondering how you'd be."

"We should have gone to your house."

If he said to her, "We still can," he'd lose her. He knew that. He might be losing her already; the door to her grief had been opened again. If she hadn't hesitated, maybe if he hadn't broken the kiss in the limousine, and they'd undressed as soon as they'd closed the front door behind them, and they were in the bed, in Kahane's bed, they might have been able to bring the significance of the moment into the lovemaking and electrified it by not denying the truth. The first time in a dead man's bed. Of course, he had more truth than she. He didn't say, "We still can." He said, "Look, let's stay up and talk, tell me about your childhood or something, and then I'll go home, and we'll go somewhere this week-end."

"Where?"

"Mexico." He said this to get through to her, to let her know that he wanted her time and that he would give her his time, his precious time. But Mexico . . . why had he volunteered Mexico?

She left her chair and came to him and gave him a long hug and cried. Griffin saw her grief. Was she crying for herself or Kahane? Would she have cried like this if a truck had run over him, or if he'd died of pneumonia? Griffin couldn't tell, but he thought not. There was something of her own confusion in the tears. Her warm forehead was like a baby's against his cheek. He stroked her hair. All he could think of saying was, "I'm sorry, baby, I'm so sorry." She broke from the hug, took a breath, and smiled at him. Her face was inches from his. He walked her to the bedroom, his arm around her waist, the friend who would soon be a lover, but not tonight. He knew that if he said, "I love you," to her, she would have said the same thing to him. She was thinking the same thoughts as he; there was no question. Almost the same thoughts. He watched her lie down on the bed, and he pulled the comforter over her.

"Thank you, Griffin," she said. "I don't know you very well, but I think you're one of the best men I've ever met. Did you mean it about Mexico?"

"Of course."

"I really need that. You don't know how much I need a change."

"We'll have a good time." He gave her a light kiss on the forehead, just long enough for her to feel the warmth of his skin.

He called a cab and waited in front of the house. A few cars passed, none slowed down, the police had gone home for the night to puzzle over his strange declamation. This seemed an interesting detail to him, that murderers didn't need to be watched as closely as thieves. Well, he said to himself, how much do you know about thieves? He wondered if he should steal something. The cab came, and he was in his own bed an hour later.

At four in the morning he woke up from his first awful dream since the murder. The dream was a terrible feeling woven through an epic of beaches, airplanes, and horses. He knew the source of this panic; here he had gone and promised June Mercator a trip to Mexico, and they were certain to be followed by the police and stopped at the airport, maybe even arrested on the plane, before it took off.

Sleep was now impossible. He went to the kitchen and made himself a hot milk and added a half inch of rum. He didn't like to drink in a crisis, but he didn't know what else to do. Cancel the trip, of course, use work as an excuse. But if he canceled, would it be as easy to sleep with June Mercator, and isn't that what he wanted? Why did he want to destroy this woman? Had he killed her lover because of the attraction he'd felt when he spoke to her on the phone the night of the murder? Would he have killed David Kahane if June Mercator had been dull on the phone?

He didn't want to cancel the trip. He could suggest San Francisco, but who cared about perfect restaurants and kissing in the fog? What would they do, drink merlot and shop for cashmere sweaters? It was heat they needed, heat he wanted, the reduction to the elements of heat, sand, salt water, suntan lotion, tequila, white cotton pants and pink shirts, high sidewalks and cobblestone streets, beggars, and the fires near the airport. There are always fires near the airport in Mexico, trash fires in the shadows of unfinished buildings.

Against the backdrop of someone else's misery he could make love to June Mercator, make love to the woman whose lover he had murdered for obscure reasons. No, obscure to a jury, clear to him still. He could make great love. There was no other place to go; fucking her in a desert resort like Palm Springs would degrade them both, it would be ugly. Kahane's ghost, if he was watching them, could justify to God the need to return in his body and haunt them if he saw them screwing where the sin was so inelegant, so predictable. Mexico and June are both unhappy, and he saw that her unhappiness would be comforted by that sad country. In Mexico he could buy her something nice, a silver ring or an old mask. It had to be Mexico.

CHAPTER FOURTEEN

Still tasting the rum, he tried to burn it away with a second glass of orange juice in the Polo Lounge. Levison was telling him that he liked June.

"You looked good together," he said.

"She's nice," said Griffin.

"How'd you come to meet a nice girl who's not in the business?"

"Friend of a friend."

"You devil, you took her from her boyfriend, didn't you?"

"Why do you say that? No."

"You're blushing."

"What am I supposed to say? I like her. We're going to Puerto Vallarta for the weekend."

"Did I give you permission to take a vacation?"

"No."

"Good, it's about time you took a trip."

Griffin brought the discussion around to work habits, and then to Larry Levy, and then to scripts and stories, and he hoped that Levison wouldn't think about June anymore.

At the office Jan gave him his messages. June had called, also Susan Avery, also Walter Stuckel, and Larry Levy, a few agents, a producer. It was strange to see, among the list of usual names, signifying usual things, the signs of the killing. June, Avery, and Stuckel stood out in relief, an esoteric design, and he was the only initiate in the cult.

He called June first, she was at work. Maybe she was backing out of the trip. He didn't want that. He was risking her arrest, and he knew he didn't care; he needed to sleep with her in a Mexican hotel room. She answered the phone.

"How does Puerto Vallarta sound?" he asked her.

"I don't know. What's it like?"

"Let's find out. Can you leave on Friday morning? Back on Monday, maybe Tuesday?"

"Can you get reservations on such short notice?"

"Yes." He could have made a light joke about the power of his office, but the seduction was beginning now, and it needed austerity and confidence. Unless he could crack her up with a joke, better to avoid an unsure attempt. He told her that Jan would call with the details.

"I had fun last night," she said.

"So did I."

Then he told Jan to book a room in Puerto Vallarta, not a high rise, and to get two round-trip first-class tickets. She asked if this was company business and he told her no.

Susan Avery was not in. Griffin left his name and then regretted it. He couldn't call back and say, "Cancel that message." No cop taking phone calls would throw away a message. Then he decided it was good he had called, if Avery was on his trail, if she had evidence, if there was a witness, he should appear calm and reasonable. Or should he be outraged? He didn't know.

Walter Stuckel was in, and he asked if he could see Griffin privately, he didn't want to talk on the phone. Griffin told him to come up. Stuckel was there in three minutes.

"I have friends in a lot of different places," said Stuckel after he shut the door.

Griffin wanted to say to him, "I'm getting tired of your act." All he was able to say, given the politics of the moment, was, "And?"

"What happened in Pasadena?"

"When?" Griffin said this softly, and he placed his voice high, to sound annoyed, hurt, mystified.

"Don't make fun of me."

"They called me in to look at mug shots." This was a perfect answer, Griffin's answer was literal; he ignored even the possibility that there was any doubt about his first visit to Pasadena. Stuckel's tone of voice called for the truth about that first visit; it trumpeted the assumption that he already knew the answer in a general way and that now, because he was Walter Stuckel and knew how to talk to people, how to make them confess, Griffin would tell him the specifics. But, of course, Griffin knew he meant what happened the night they screened *The Bicycle Thief* at the Rialto. Griffin would never answer that question.

"Mug shots?" Griffin couldn't tell if Stuckel knew about the visit to Avery. He must; otherwise, this meeting made no sense.

"Yes, in case I recognized anyone who might have been in Pasadena the night that writer was killed." *That writer*—this was a good touch, and Stuckel was already being put off-balance. "It was fascinating. It was just like the movies."

"What happened?"

"Well, I think they have someone who saw what happened from a distance, but he, or she, didn't get a good look at the killer. That's why you're here, isn't it? You know something."

"There's a chance they think it was you."

"That I killed the guy?"

"You fit the description."

"They haven't said anything to me."

"Of course not."

"Well, aren't you supposed to know your accusers?"

"Maybe you should get a lawyer."

"Why?"

"In case they come for you."

"I had a drink with the guy, Walter, that's all. This is ridiculous."

"If you went to Pasadena with the intent to kill, you could go to the gas chamber."

Griffin held back a smile; this was starting to sound like *Habeas Corpus*. "I went to Pasadena with the intent to hire."

"That's what you keep saying."

"Why would I have killed him?"

"I'm just telling you what they think."

After Walter left, the travel agent called to give Griffin the itinerary for the trip. She'd found a second-floor room at an older hotel, with a view of the beach. Griffin called June and told her to be packed by seven A.M. He thought of asking her to dinner the night before they left; he could cancel an old appointment, but he didn't want to sleep with her until they were in Mexico, and there was no point in going to dinner now without going to bed afterward. It would be the most romantic if they flew on separate planes and met for dinner in a bar overlooking the Pacific, but maybe there was a way to make checking in romantic. Well, they were going first-class, so she'd be studiously casual about the better service. If they sold perfume duty-free on the plane, he'd buy her some. He'd ask her to put it on, in the plane. She'd resist, he'd insist, and he'd smell it, he'd put his face to her neck. And he'd pay people to carry the bags, he'd hire a taxi, he wouldn't take the hotel bus, he'd keep June apart from the tourists. He would treat her like a movie star.

He watched the lights on his phone. One line was blinking; someone was on hold. One line lit up for a moment and then went off; someone had left a message, or reached a wrong number, or Jan had picked up the phone and reached a busy signal. One line had been on for five minutes; Jan was probably talking to a friend. He could lift the receiver and listen in, but this was something he had never done, never even considered. He wondered why this had never occurred to him before. Did it mean he wasn't really interested in Jan, or that he was too busy to pry into her life, or that he was moral? But how can you be moral if you've never faced temptation? Was he tempted to listen in on Jan? He put his hand on the receiver and punched the button next to her line. He lifted the receiver a quarter of an inch and then set it back in place. He renounced the urge.

A producer came in with two writers, brothers. They'd written a few dozen television episodes and then a screenplay, which Levison had read; as a favor he'd read the script and not the coverage. The story they pitched to Griffin was not fully worked out, and the producer kept jumping in to assure Griffin that filling in the holes was merely technical.

They all knew that Griffin was passing on it. The writers were happy, though; they had a lot of money from their television work and they were learning how to make the transition to movies. The producer looked unhappy. Griffin wondered how the writers' agent had connected them with this producer, who needed them more than they needed him; his last movie had been awful, had destroyed the career of the star, an actress who proved herself so inept in light comedy, so ungainly, that no one would consider her for the romantic parts for which she had earned her stripes. As they left the room, the producer looked to Griffin. "Well, what do you think?"

"I'll get back to you," he said.

The phone rang. It was Bonnie Sherow. "How are you?" she asked.

"When did you get back?"

"This morning. What are you doing this weekend?"

"The weekend isn't good."

"I wanted to go away with you." She didn't even question what he was doing, it was unreasonable to expect him to be free on short notice.

He had to clear himself completely. He pretended to be looking at his calendar. "How about dinner on Saturday? No, shit, I've got this distributor from Australia coming in, I'm supposed to talk about a deal with him. Maybe the weekend after."

"No, my mother's coming into town."

"The weekend after that, then."

"Let's try it."

"How did it go with the book?"

"We got it."

"Congratulations." He was jealous. He had expected her to lose the book. Why hadn't he told her that he was going to Mexico with another woman? Why couldn't he just stop it with Bonnie? He was so used to lying that he had lied without thinking. For once the truth would help, it could release him from this dead love affair. He could tell her, but then she'd ask too many questions about June. Someone would probably tell her that Griffin had been with June at the ball the night before. He couldn't say anything vague to Bonnie, she wouldn't let him say that June had been introduced by a friend, she'd want to know which friend and how did the friend know June.

Levy called to say that the deal was closed with Oakley and Civella. Oakley was getting eighty thousand for a first draft and a set of revisions, against three hundred and seventy-five thousand if he directed the picture, and two hundred thousand if he didn't. Oakley's agent had demanded that he be pay or play, that the studio pay him the full two hundred whether or not the studio made the movie, but he caved in when told that this was a deal-breaker. If Oakley believed so much in the script, he could write it at home and put it up for auction when he finished. Civella would get twenty thousand to supervise the writing, and both would be given offices.

Susan Avery returned the call as Griffin was on his way to lunch. As he took the phone, he considered that he could still go to Mexico with June without the police knowing about it.

"Hello, Miss Avery. Have you found him yet?"

"I can't really discuss an ongoing investigation, Mr. Mill."

"Well, if I can be of any help . . ."

"How long have you known June Mercator?"

"About a month."

"Since you went to Pasadena."

"Since David Kahane died, yes."

"You didn't know her before that date?"

"We met over the phone, actually. We started talking and felt very comfortable together. We talked about that feeling, and then one conversation led to another. She thought that I might have special information, that you might tell me more than you'd tell her, because of my position."

"You've been out with her."

"Yes, we've been out."

"You don't think it's a little too soon for her to go out in public?"

"This isn't Iran, Miss Avery. I don't think women are bound by a special set of rules. She hasn't recovered from the loss of the man she loved. I'm there for her as a friend, that's all. Actually, well, there is a special feeling between us. I think both of us feel that we're on to something real." He hoped this made him sound too dumb to have planned a crime of passion. "Of course, you can call her. I'm sure she'll be happy to pick over the horror of what happened to her. I'm sure that's what she needs." Now his outrage felt appropriate. This is what an innocent man would do.

What would happen if he hung up on her, if he slammed the phone down? No one did that to the police. Would such an overreaction, such indignation, prove his guilt? The risk was too great, the calculations had already taken too long, Avery's three seconds of silence meant that her conscience had checked her ambition and found it a little keen. She didn't want to make a widow cry. The pause meant she wouldn't call June.

"You have to understand," said Avery, "that a murder investigation is sometimes, and necessarily, unpleasant. The bad guys don't do us favors."

"Look, I'm sorry if I sound impatient, but all I did was see a man a little while before he was mugged and murdered, and I've helped you as much as I could, and I'll help you as much as I can, but I don't feel that I'm getting any thanks, and I guess I should know, considering the business I'm in, that someone as overworked as you doesn't have time to hold everyone's hand any more than I do." Griffin wasn't sure what he had said or why, but he thought he was letting them both off the hook.

"And we appreciate that help, Griffin."

As soon as she said good-bye, he wanted to erase the entire conversation. He'd made a terrible mistake. By telling him that she knew he had been out with June, she was letting him know they'd been tailed. He hadn't said anything to her about the cop who had tagged after him through the hotel, which would suggest to Avery that he wasn't surprised at being followed, which would mean only one thing, that he was expecting the tail. And why would he expect to be followed if he wasn't guilty? But what could he have said? Avery hadn't mentioned it. He might have said, "By the way, Susan, something strange happened last night, and maybe it's related." No. She didn't know for sure that he knew he had been followed by the Pasadena police. So he had done the right thing by not bringing it up. Should he have asked her how she had known that he had been out with June? It was impossible to know.

And still he wanted to take June Mercator to Mexico? Griffin thought, for the first time, that perhaps he was insane. He opened a drawer and looked at the small pile of postcards from the Writer. The Writer was probably a loner, didn't have many friends, and those he did surely thought of him as crazy. No one who sends anonymous postcards with death threats, who shoots to kill in alleys, who leaves obscure messages on ballroom tables can walk through life without a trail of shattered friendships. Rage, long ruminations, little insults, or teases mulled over during hours of fruitless labor at the typewriter or at the computer, staring at the cursor as it demands the next letter, the next word; of course the Writer chewed through affection.

He drove to Beverly Hills and lunched with Dick Mellen at The Grill. He wanted to ask him if he knew a good criminal lawyer, thought of asking him as though he were researching something for a movie but held back. He told him he was going to Mexico for a few days.

"That's a good idea, you look like you could use the rest."

"Really?" Griffin wanted to know if the strain showed. "Well, work's been frantic the last few weeks." This was a standard lament, meaning nothing. Everyone in the restaurant was under pressure, the work wasn't easy for anyone, they were all veterans of the long day, and yet here they were, smiling, sitting up nicely in their booths and at their tables, shoulders relaxed, eyes keeping contact, except to scan the room for friends or celebrities, or better still, celebrities who were friends. The eager friendliness shined from every corner of the room. Why? Because no one was paying for their meals, everyone was on an expense allowance? Or because everyone made so much money? There were a few writers and directors sitting with studio executives, Griffin's rank or one notch below at other companies, and even these were caught in the mood of the room. Everyone wore cotton, or cotton and silk, or linen. Everyone was clean. It would be different in prison. Would Griffin make a joke of calling the dining hall the commissary? Would his cell mates think he was funny if he pretended that he was still on the outside? He hoped there would be a place in prison where the men with power met, only the brightest and coolest, some corner of the yard where the air was thin and the posture was sharp. Will they respect my crime? he wondered.

He shook some hands on his way out of the restaurant and drove back to the studio slowly, taking Laurel Canyon instead of the freeway; he was lingering. If the police arrested him, he might be denied bail, now that he held tickets for Mexico. He might never see Laurel Canyon again. He stopped on Mulholland Drive and looked at the Valley. He felt a gush of stupid sentimentality for a section of the world he usually despised. It wasn't their fault, everyone who lived on this plain; they had to live somewhere. And they chose a place that everyone made fun of, so perhaps they were pioneers, deserving respect. If these minor people read about Griffin's trial in the paper, or saw it on television, they would condemn him.

Last night's bad dream came back to him, and he wished he hadn't killed David Kahane. If he went to prison, he knew he would think about the murder every day until they gassed him. He started the car and drove back to the studio, staying away from the boulevards; he didn't want to look at people shopping, he wanted to pass through residential neighborhoods. He wanted to look at houses. He saw mothers and babies, people watering their lawns. At a stoplight he saw the driver of the car beside him staring at him. Why not? Griffin was crying.

CHAPTER FIFTEEN

Levison formally introduced Larry Levy to the production team. Everyone grinned, and Levy was the most satisifed in the group. Griffin watched the faces of the others, but no one betrayed their suspicion of the new boy, or fear for their jobs. Perhaps their lawyers were already searching around town for new jobs, but if their lawyers were smart—and Griffin knew most of their lawyers—they had cautioned their clients not to bolt, or even to appear to bolt. So what were they telling themselves, that Levy had little power yet, that he had not been hired with a mandate to clean house? The company had been through a bloodletting four years ago; Levison and then Levison and Mill had made money for the company. Did they really believe that Levy was there to help out, not to take over? Of course he was there to take over, and yes, their jobs were all in danger. There would be no verdict on him for another three months, when the scripts he had developed began coming in, but before then there would be meetings to talk about what to start up, there would be long arguments about directors, there would be story conferences where someone could always frighten the others with brilliance, make them scared to speak out, if he was properly caustic, confident, and right. Did Griffin have the energy anymore to beat back that kind of personality?

Everyone spoke about their projects. Now the fear showed itself. Even Levison was left to one side while the vice-presidents and the story editors told Levy the status of their scripts. Levy had nothing to say about the two films that were in production. There were fifty-five different scripts being written for the studio as of the meeting, with two deals closed in the last week, including Tom Oakley's. Levison had recently assigned Alison Kelly, the story editor, the job of reading all the coverage written for each executive each week, and she described her job and her criteria. Levy asked a few simple questions during the presentations; obviously he'd thought about this meeting and had decided not to grandstand. Of course, Levy was scared, too, and didn't want to commit himself to a strong opinion about anything at this first meeting. He asked to read a few scripts, but with each request he added, "If you don't mind" or, "I'm curious to see what they're doing with the material." It become obvious to Griffin, if not to the others, that Levy would not personally attack anyone. He would go to Levison over the next two months and tell him that Alison was useless, or that someone's eight scripts were all dreadful, or that someone else didn't have the line to such and such a director and that the studio was heading toward a repeat of the previous year, only two hits, one a sequel, and one with Spielberg; nothing developed in-house had done well.

The meeting, which began at two-thirty, ended at seven. Griffin checked his office. Jan was gone, she'd left his message list, she'd told everyone he would be away for a few days and that he'd call after the weekend. The tickets and the hotel reservation slip was in her desk. He looked around the office, thinking that if they arrested him at the airport, he might not see this place again.

In the parking lot he said good night to Alison Kelly. She was going back to Beverly Hills for a screening at the Academy Theater. Griffin said he'd be there, but going over the canyon, he changed his mind and went home.

He called Jacopo's for a pizza and then called them back and canceled the order. He opened a can of smoked oysters and a box of Triscuits and ate the oysters one at a time on a Triscuit, making a sandwich of two oysters between two Triscuits when the can was almost finished. He drank a large Perrier from the bottle. His brain had stopped, he realized. There was no grand plan working away, his fear had either subsided or had frozen him, he couldn't say. If this was depression, he'd never felt it before. He thought that if someone put a pin in his hand, he wouldn't know about it for a day. He couldn't imagine bleeding.

The phone rang. It was the Writer.

"Don't think I'm going to let you get away with this." The voice started deep but broke in the middle of the sentence. Where was he from? New York? Baltimore? Maybe. He had the slightly nasal sound of Baltimore, mixed with an edge of undeserved pride.

"With what?" asked Griffin.

"With destroying people's lives."

"I don't know what you're talking about." A few days ago Griffin might have thrown up in fear if he'd thought that the Writer had seen him kill Kahane; now he didn't panic at all.

"Why are you people always so smug? Where do you get off being so self-satisfied?"

"I guess it's because we like our work, and because our work is hard."

"Don't tell me you think you work hard."

"If I hang up, you'll call me right back, won't you?"

"That's right."

"Don't you think it's time to end this game?"

"No, I don't."

"Look, I know you think this is the most creative thing you've ever done, but why not sit down and write a screenplay without asking for money up front?"

"Yeah, I knew you'd say something like that. That's not the issue. The issue is, you owed me a phone call, you owed me a word."

"Well, I'm sorry. Okay? I am sorry. I've said it, I mean it, and now you'll never call me again. Thank you." Griffin hung up. He immediately called June Mercator and confirmed what time he'd pick her up. Then he packed and went to bed.

He gave himself up to the familiar darkness and thought of the Writer. He was terribly unsatisfying, thought Griffin. He was smart that way, he offered no rhythm. He was anywhere he wanted to be, it seemed, and he interrupted Griffin's life in a random way that always put Griffin on the defensive. He had wanted to cause Griffin trouble and he had, more than he would ever know. He'd had his revenge.

That night Griffin couldn't sleep. He lay in bed, willing himself to get up and at least read a script or drink a glass of warm milk, but something strong defeated his will. What was it? He imagined his skin covered with a light blue flame; all the static electricity he'd built up since the killing was now ready to spark. For a moment he thought he'd suffered a stroke; his brain was terribly alive but his body was frozen, he wanted to scream but his mouth wouldn't open. There wasn't even any tension, there was just a collapsed line between his brain and his muscles. Was it really only a moment, or did the aphasia last the night? When he could finally move, the sun was up.

He packed quickly and waited for the limousine.

Griffin watched June's face as she opened her front door, her eyes focused over his shoulder, on the long black car. She brought them back to Griffin and kissed him on the lips.

"You ready?" he asked.

"I can't tell you how glad I am that we're doing this."

The limousine driver came up the walk to carry June's suitcase. Bonnie Sherow traveled with three pieces of luggage. June's two-suiter was light enough to carry on the plane, it was lighter than Griffin's. Here was another reason to love her: She didn't need much.

She wore white cotton pants and an expensive pink T-shirt, a green sweater over her back with the arms tied loosely around her neck, and when she slipped into the limousine—like an expert, Griffin thought—she put on mirrored sunglasses. On her feet were black high-topped sneakers. The whole blend, read piece by piece, declared a modest but sincere attempt to be independent of the country club. The sunglasses and the sneakers battled the green sweater and the white pants. Griffin found himself with his arm around her before he could think about it, and he gently bit her shoulder.

At the airport the driver carried the bags to the first-class counter. Griffin looked around the terminal, wondering who the cop was. It was impossible to tell. How would they know he was going to Mexico? If Susan Avery called his office today, he would already be in Mexican airspace.

As they approached the gate, Griffin began to sweat. Yes, and his heart started to pound. It was the worst he had ever felt without being sick; if this had been the walk to the gas chamber, he couldn't imagine feeling a deeper sense of hollow, bleak terror, and loss without bottom. And June couldn't sense it! He was sure the gate attendant knew to call the police when Griffin presented the ticket.

No. They were walking down the jet way to the plane.

He was sure the stewardess was supposed to call the police once he had locked his seat belt.

No. She brought him a margarita. He waved his hand, to tell her that he never drank this early in the day, but June slapped his hand down and he heard her say, "This is a vacation, you have to have it." He tried to smile, but he wanted to cry. As the crew shut the doors, as the plane backed away from the terminal, Griffin looked out the window for a police car, probably an unmarked car, but there were only baggage carts, fuel tankers, and food-service trucks.

He sipped the margarita, hoping that the tequila would steady him, but it seemed as though the alcohol were going to someone else's brain, not his. Griffin the murderer was clear, some other Griffin, the man on vacation with a pretty woman was starting to have fun, but he was in a different universe from the Griffin who watched the ocean as the plane banked to the south and made a left turn toward Mexico. In the tourist cabin, a group of college boys let out movie-bandito yells.

At some point—Griffin wasn't sure when—maybe ten minutes into the flight, he heard June ask him what was the matter.

"Actually I'm afraid of flying," he said. Could he really expect her to believe him? He needed sympathy, and the fear of planes created the kind of unreasonable panic that generated the same kind of horrible feelings he had now, so that he could tell her a history of this phobia, she could talk him through it, and even though she was not addressing the real cause of his misery, still, he could simulate a misery she would be glad to soothe. He would steal her sympathy.

"What's it like, what do you feel like right now?"

"I feel like I just dropped some bad acid."

"I never tripped."

"Well, it's the opposite of fun."

"Tell me about it."

"I always hated tripping." He started to tell her about a bad trip when he was in high school, a true story. What a relief that he didn't have to lie about a fear of flying, and he didn't have to tell her that he was scared of everyone right now, since he was sure that at any moment someone would arrest both of them for the murder of her lover.

The flight attendants brought more drinks and food, and hot towels. Griffin was able to tell June exactly how he felt, without telling her why. As they wiped their faces with the hot towels, Griffin said that when he used to trip, he was always grateful for kindnesses, desperate to find them anywhere, and the smallest generosity was proof of God's grace. So a visit to an ice-cream store yielded a miracle when the girl behind the counter gave him a taste of a flavor.

"But they always do that," said June.

"Yes, but when you're tripping, the ordinary takes on tremendous weight, everything fits into the divine plan."

"So what happens on bad trips? Does everything convince you that the devil is alive?"

"Yes," he said as she took his hand and kissed it. Trees were at eye level. They landed in Puerto Vallarta.

Getting off a plane in the tropics was one of Griffin's favorite moments. He liked the stairs that rolled out to meet the jet; he liked the passengers, wearing their new sunglasses, running across the tarmac to be the first inside the cool terminal where the baggage was slow to arrive; he liked the brown workers; and he liked that combination of relaxation and police terror. There were men in uniforms, some with machine guns, but Griffin's fear, dissolved by June's tender comfort, was nothing more than a thin mist. Was the bad trip over? Or was this still the trip, a false dawn? Would he collapse in the hotel room?

While they waited for their bags, he thought he was being watched by a customs official. The official, at his station near the end of the baggage-claim area, looked at Griffin without pretending to look elsewhere. Griffin was his target. It was almost noon, eleven in Los Angeles; Susan Avery would have had time to speak to Jan, find out where Griffin was, and the call . . . call who? The FBI? The Treasury Department? Of course there was a liaison office working with local police departments, but could they locate him so quickly? Would he rate such swift pursuit? It seemed unlikely. Unless there was a warrant out for him. If a court had ordered his arrest, then maybe the Mexicans would cooperate within an hour. He was easy to find. Jan knew the flight number, and the airport was small. June lifted her bag from the conveyor belt, and he followed her to the checkout line. They were directed away from the official who was looking at him. He was behind Griffin during baggage inspection and passport control. When their official let them through, Griffin looked back at the one who had been staring at him. He was gone.

June spoke Spanish to the cabdriver on the way to the hotel. She spoke it as well as David Kahane had spoken Japanese, without hesitation, and she was casual about her slightly flattened accent. When the driver stopped talking to concentrate on the road, Griffin asked her what they'd talked about. It was about politics. She showed Griffin the graffiti for a candidate. Griffin had been jealous of her lover, and now he was jealous of her. It bothered him that he didn't speak another language, and he hated himself for his ignorance of Mexican politics. Suddenly a knowledge of Mexican politics seemed the most crucial information a man could possibly own; without a detailed understanding of the political history of this country, Griffin knew he was uncivilized, a barbarian.

"Do you speak any other languages?" Griffin asked.

"French, and a little Japanese."

"Where'd you get that?"

"I got the French and Spanish in high school, I got the Japanese when I was in college. I spent a semester in Kyoto. That's how I met David. David spoke beautiful Japanese."

He almost said, "I know." Instead he let her sentence lie there, he didn't pick it up, didn't respond, he held his breath for half a minute, following the sweep hand on his watch. The second use of David's name was full of memory. He let his breath out when they saw the hotel.

June was happy. She said just enough to show she liked the hotel without saying too many words, without gushing over the architecture. The hotel was white, low, with palms and bouganvillea, two swimming pools, a thatched bar between the pools, and a long thatched bar at the beach. It wasn't the most expensive hotel in Puerto Vallarta, and Griffin thought that that was better. No one here would know him. If he stayed at the top place, he would be sure to find a producer he knew, or an agent. The more money he spent, the harder it was to hide.

Their room had a balcony, and from the bed the view was of tiled roof, thatching, and palm trees. It was perfect. Griffin compared June to Bonnie Sherow. When Bonnie came into the room in Cabo San Lucas, she talked about how she felt like a grown-up, and this had made Griffin hate her. June went to the refrigerator. One side was a bar. She opened a small bottle of tequila. What he liked about the gesture was the way she did it without having to say that the bottle would cost money, because the hotel stocked the bar and someone counted the bottles every morning. She spent his money and didn't ask his permission. Yes, it was good to get a little drunk on a weekday afternoon with a woman he had not yet slept with.

He liked her for changing into her bathing suit in the bathroom. She wasn't skinny. The waist he felt when holding her was wide and high. And wasn't he now fifteen pounds too heavy, probably twenty? She saw him looking at her.

"Come on, fat boy," she said, gripping his tummy with her fingers, "Let's get a tan."

Griffin hoped he would always remember that afternoon on the beach in Puerto Vallarta. In a few days he would probably be in jail, and he might never again look out over his belly to the sea. Everything was precious. He saw himself at seventy, serving his life term if he didn't go to the gas chamber, boring his cell mate with the story of his Mexican fling.

"June bought a straw hat from a beach vendor," he would say. "And then a man with a tray of silver jewelry rushed to us as soon as June opened her purse. I was ready to tell him to go away, but I liked some earrings, thin spikes in a circle, and bought them. I knew she'd wear them only on this weekend, and that made them even more wonderful. A waiter from the bar came around taking drink orders, and we both asked for margaritas. Before the drinks arrived, she took my hand and dragged me into the warm bay. We floated on our backs and let the waves carry us up to the margin of sea and beach, where it was dry. We had to run back into the water to wash the sand from our bathing suits. Then we drank the margaritas and read magazines."

Maybe he wouldn't tell anyone the story, maybe he would keep it a secret. It was the kind of story he'd repeat, though he hated people who kept a portfolio of stories, people who turned their lives into a routine. He didn't want to be pathetic.

There were two Mexican policemen on the beach. Griffin didn't know how long they'd been there. Both wore khaki shirts and pants, and stiff black leather holsters at their waists. Was this normal, or for him? If he was the government, he would prefer to watch Griffin and hope he'd return to Los Angeles on his own. Was an extradition fight good for tourism? Did it matter at all? The policemen joked with a few vendors. June said she was going back to the room. Griffin told her he'd be along in a few minutes, he wanted to watch the water. She kissed him on the lips, twice.

As she walked away, one of the policemen followed her, and the other watched Griffin. Would they let him change before taking him to the police station? Would he be beaten in his bathing suit and his rubber sandals? Could he bribe them? He felt the panic from the airplane again. If June was under arrest now, she would have no idea why; the charge would seem insane. Griffin would deny it, too, of course, and why should she not believe him? The indictment would have to say that the two knew each other before the murder; otherwise, how could a jury believe that they had planned this together? Griffin could save her if her lawyer couldn't prove that they didn't know each other. If the lawyer couldn't see what was obviously June's best defense, Griffin would send him a note, anonymously, to alert the lawyer to the winning strategy.

Griffin imagined what would happen if he was arrested in Mexico. The Los Angeles Police, or the Pasadena Police, would get a search warrant for his apartment, and then they would find the postcards, just as they would have found them if the Writer's aim had been true in the alley in

Beverly Hills. What would have happened then? They might have traced the postcards back to Griffin's killer. Griffin stopped himself from following this track, it was a waste of time. He could always think about this in prison.

He felt sorry for June. Even if June's lawyer helped her without one error, the case was too juicy to go unnoticed, they'd be celebrity killers in every paper in America. Who knows if someone on the beach wasn't taking pictures of them with a hidden camera, to sell to a news service? Their paunches might be famous. June could never recover from the suspicion, even if Griffin declared on the stand that he acted alone, and used some kind of insanity plea, with the postcards as the key to explain the paranoia that had led to a senseless killing. No one—no lawyer, no jury, no press agent—could recover June's innocence. The arrest would destroy her right to grieve Kahane's death in her own way; reporters would find the people she worked with, they'd say she bounced back too quickly from his murder, not a month later and she was in Mexico with his killer! Maybe a good prosecuter could prove to a jury that even without tangible evidence, motel receipts, telephone bills, it is still reasonable to assume that Griffin and June had known each other for a long time before the killings, because it was entirely unreasonable to imagine that she would fall so quickly in love with a man who claimed to have seen her for the first time at Kahane's funeral. The truth was more sordid than the lie that could send her to jail. A trip to Puerto Vallarta! Margaritas on the beach! Guilty, guilty, guilty.

Someone would buy the rights to the story, once they were both in jail. It wouldn't be a movie, it was the sort of morality play that television liked to put on, they'd spread it over two nights, they'd make a big meal of the trial. Monday night, the affair with June and the murder of Kahane. Tuesday night, the brilliant work by Susan Avery. All the cat-and-mouse games with her, they'd be good for a half hour of screen time. What would they start with? Griffin would begin the show with Kahane's pitch. How would they construct the first meeting with June, what would the jury think had happened? They'd have to show him meeting June before he killed Kahane. He'd have to have slept with June before the murder too. The phone call from June telling him that Kahane was at the movies. The trip to Pasadena—would they include the Japanese piano bar? That would make a nice scene, thought Griffin, although it was probably too subtle for television. And who would play Griffin? Michael Douglas? Val Kilmer would be terrific, thought Griffin, he could play the office politician, the smarm, the manipulator. Or John Malkovich? He could play the paranoid. And what if they told the story as it happened? How would they figure in the postcards? Would they be lost in the story? If Griffin killed for love, then the postcards didn't fit. If Griffin killed because he was crazy, then passion didn't fit. Would the actress play June as if she were innocent or guilty? What an awful moment, when June gets arrested and has no idea what is happening. When she is fingerprinted and photographed. When she is put into a cell until a friend or her father bails her out. And the first conversation with Griffin, is he out on bail too? No. Having left the country once, they'd be seen as risks, bail would either be too high for anyone to pay, or else bail would be denied. When would they see each other? Of course they wouldn't share lawyers, they wouldn't share strategies, so they wouldn't see each other again until and unless they were tried together. And if they weren't tried together, maybe he'd never see her again, as long as he lived. If the television movie of his crime told the truth, would they know about the gunshots in the alley? Of course. The police would find out everything.

Would they find out who sent the postcards?

What would the Writer do when Griffin was charged with a writer's murder? He would know everything, as soon as the postcards were introduced in court or mentioned on the news. He might even be the best choice to write the script. No. With the publication of the postcards there would be a hunt for him. He would be famous as the creep who drove the executive to murder. Would anyone have sympathy with his private war against Griffin? Griffin was stirred by a hopeful thought: He could prove that the Writer's pursuit had passed over from the mail to direct violence. There was the gunplay in the alley. No one knew about that except Griffin and the Beverly Hills Police. They must have known that the shattered glass in the alley was from a Mercedes, and Griffin had the receipt from the auto-glass shop. More trouble for Griffin, of course; why hadn't he gone directly to the police as soon as he was shot at? Yes, why hadn't he? How could they have connected the alley with Kahane? Griffin couldn't remember what his reason had been, unless he was afraid that Walter Stuckel would make the connection, but what was there to see, what was the pattern? Dead writer, and executive shot at in an alley. It would have been easy to get out of, no reason for anyone to hear about it. If they'd asked him why he'd been driving in the alley, he could have told them he was using an old shortcut, he'd thought of going to Santa Monica Boulevard, four long blocks south, but had changed his mind and turned back to Sunset. No. They wouldn't have liked that answer. There is no good reason on earth not to run to the police when someone shoots at you unless you have something to hide. If he tried to lie, they would ask him about the postcard delivered to his table at the Beverly Hills Hotel. How would they know about that card? They would have gone to the hotel to find out if he'd been in any kind of fight.

Griffin watched the Mexican policeman, the vendors, the tourists, the sea, a cruise ship, the clouds. He had made too many mistakes. He had lied to too many people. When the first card arrived, no, when the third card arrived, the card with the death threat, he should have gone straight to Walter Stuckel, straight to Levison, and showed it to them. He should have asked for help. He shouldn't have worried about the cards' effect on his job. And now it was too late to show the cards to anyone.

What if the Writer didn't have an alibi for the night of Kahane's murder? Could Griffin get him blamed for the killing? Impossible. It was a desperate thought, and Griffin felt shame for it.

The beach was almost empty now. The vendors were gone. A few drunk couples sat at the thatched bar, waiting for the sunset. The Mexican policeman was gone. When had he left? Griffin stood up, feeling dizzy. He picked up his towel, his sandals, his magazines. In a comedy these details could make an audience laugh, or at least set the character as fussy, someone the audience had no need to take seriously. Griffin walked back to the room, hating himself, feeling sorry for himself, and then hating himself for the self-pity. He worked so hard that he never really had the time or the need to take his emotional temperature; surely that was one reason he'd taken no vacations for so many years, anything to avoid a long look at who he was. The Writer wouldn't understand that, he wouldn't believe that Griffin had an unconscious, like anyone's, the usual cesspool.

June called to him from the balcony as he walked through the gardens by their wing.

"There's a message for you."

"Oh, no, we haven't even been here six hours."

"It's from your lawyer."

"I'll be right up."

Before he knocked on the door, he let out as long a breath as he could, and then breathed in slowly. He smiled hard and tapped on the door. June opened it, wearing a white T-shirt and tan shorts. Her knees and shins were pink from the sun, but it didn't look painful. She gave him the message pad, but he knew the number. He called the hotel operator, and she put him through immediately. It annoyed him that she didn't have to take the number and call him back when she made the connection; he needed an illusion of distance to stay sane.

He spoke to his lawyer's secretary. He was gone for the day.

"Do you know what this was about?"

"Sorry, Griffin."

The connection was perfect; she might have been downstairs. What is it, fiber optics? he asked himself, and then answered, Don't think about this now. "Does he want me to come back?"

"I don't think so."

"He didn't leave a message for me in case I called?"

He saw June watching him. He had to let the panic go. He breathed out another lump of unhappy air.

"Griffin, you're on vacation. Call him tomorow morning." Griffin always forgot her name, and she was always so casual with him.

"Everything's okay?" He couldn't stop.

"Griffin, you're in Mexico, go get drunk." It was the style of some secretaries to assume great ease with him, playing the wise sister. He knew she knew what the call was about, but for all the friendliness, she was not a friend, she was a woman careful of her job, and she would never tell him. Besides, he could never remember her name. He said good-bye. She said, *"Adios."*

He put the phone down.

"What did he want?" asked June.

"I don't know. He's gone for the day."

"Do you think it's important?" She wanted it to be important, she liked the idea that the long arm of the movies reached him at an instant, anywhere. It made her weekend more interesting, he was that much more impressive.

"I'm not going back until Monday." He took off his rubber sandals. As he stood up, he could see over the balcony to the garden below. The policeman who had followed June was there, resting against a palm tree, smoking a cigarette. "Let me take a shower," he said, "and then we'll see the town."

CHAPTER SIXTEEN

She wore a white cotton dress, some kind of knit. Griffin always wanted to call it jersey, but he wasn't sure. She wore the silver earrings from the beach. He didn't know her perfume, but it was flowery, young. Bonnie Sherow wore something heavier; why didn't he know the names of these things? He supposed Bonnie's perfumes were more sophisticated than June's, but the ordinary, the popular, made him happy so often. To be part of everyday life, to be part of the flow. Why else work in the movies?

They walked along the waterfront avenue in the town. There were droves of college kids everywhere, most of them drunk, sitting at tables in bars that were made to look like Mexican cantinas. Fake Mexico in Mexico, because the owner was a fan of *The Treasure of the Sierra Madre*. Everything was a stage set now.

June told him her life story. She was adopted. This upset him, he had orphaned her a second time. She grew up in Philadelphia, went to private school in Maryland, college in Vermont, the semester in Japan, then to New York, a job with a magazine, a boyfriend had moved to Los Angeles, she followed, they broke up, she ran into Kahane, she got the job at the bank, that was two years ago. She was twenty-nine. She loved her father and spoke of him with respect. He was some kind of moderate tycoon, a powerful athlete, a great host. She fought with her mother. She had a brother at Stanford Law. Her parents' natural child. Yes, there was some resentment.

They ate a bad meal at a large restaurant, and then walked some more, up the streets that led to the hill overlooking the town, behind a big church.

Griffin looked around and was sure the police had stopped following them after they'd left the hotel. As they climbed a steep set of stairs, he turned June to him and pinned her to the locked gate over the door of a liquor store.

"What are you doing?" she asked, but she knew.

The kiss scared him. It might have been the best of his life, it might have been the first time he'd ever really kissed someone as an equal. What was it? Was it Kahane or was it June? Was he tasting the man he'd killed, or was she tasting the killer and, through him, her dead lover? He realized that she was larger and taller than most of the women he'd ever kissed, larger than Bonnie Sherow. He'd slept with actresses, but they usually curled into him, looking for protection. There were delicate women with thin bones who received him, but he always felt like a trespasser. Yes, Kahane was between them now; they were both kissing something between them, a ghost, something they shared. They were on the same side of the mirror. He could do anything. He lifted her dress, she kissed him harder. He put his hands in her underpants, she grabbed his shoulders. He stopped. She took his arm and they continued up the stairs. They turned down a new street. He pressed her into a doorway and unbuttoned his fly. He pulled her dress up above her waist and rubbed himself against her wide, soft belly. He wasn't sure if she could come in this position, and he lowered her dress.

"What's wrong?" she asked. Was she willing to let him come against her in the alley? Yes.

"Let's go back to the hotel." He knew she thought he was scared of lying down in the street.

In the room he poured mineral water into champagne glasses and walked to the balcony, looking for the police. The garden was empty. June hugged him from behind and hooked her chin over his shoulder. He brought a hand to her leg and gathered her dress in his fingers, pulling it up until he could slip into her underpants again.

They lay on the bed and watched the tops of the palms, and the roof beyond the garden. It was hot in the room.

"Let me turn on the air conditioner," he said.

"No. I like it like this. Don't you?"

"Yes."

Bonnie would have turned on the air conditioner. Bonnie would have taken a shower as soon as they came back. Bonnie wouldn't have let him jack off against her stomach in a Mexican alley in the middle of the night.

They held their silly, fat bodies together and sweated. He didn't want to go inside her. He stroked her with his hand, softly, and she came. He let her rest, and then he helped her come again. She pushed him onto his back, and he watched her watching him. It was a look between life-forms, between two bodies of organized cells, and he tried to let her see the murder in his eyes. She kissed him, and he supposed that all she saw was pain.

He rolled her onto her stomach and stretched himself along her back. Sliding on the sweat between them, he came. Bonnie would have made a joke about the sperm dribbling down her back, she would have wiped it off immediately. June let him stay where he was. He watched the sperm slide over her waist to the bed.

Well, he thought, maybe my cell mates will ask to hear the story again. They'll ask me why I didn't fuck her. What will I say? It was enough. As it was, we stayed equals. I didn't need to penetrate. He expected the cell mates to offer another explanation, one he'd already considered, that he couldn't share the same space with David Kahane, he was scared of the ghost. Maybe he couldn't because he didn't want to spoil her any more than he already had, that after his arrest he wanted to leave her with something intact, so she could love other men. No, he was not so generous, it was the first reason, and he smiled when he thought of a phrase sure to make a cell mate laugh: He couldn't park his car in Kahane's garage.

He called Dick Mellen at home in the morning. The service answered and said he was out of town for the weekend. They didn't know where he'd gone, but he usually checked in for messages in the late afternoon. If Mellen's first call had been about the police, about an arrest, he would have made sure to get through to him by now, Griffin thought, so whatever he wanted was important but could wait until Monday. So it must be about work, and Griffin ran through the possibilities. He was fired. He was being offered a job somewhere else. Maybe Mellen was leaving this firm and was calling to ask if Griffin would go with him to a new one. No, he wouldn't call Griffin on his vacation with that kind of news, and of course Griffin would stay with him. Levison is leaving the studio. That was possible. Larry Levy is taking over. That was not possible, not yet. His lawyer was calling simply to tell him to have a good time, to recommend a restaurant or a beach. That was possible too. Griffin wondered how he could survive the weekend, followed by the Mexican police, without knowing what the call was about. There was all of Saturday and Sunday ahead of them. He could pretend that he'd made the call to the lawyer from the hotel's office, and say that he was needed back in town for some kind of high-level studio meeting on Sunday, she'd believe that. But the police who were watching him were probably waiting for him to go home. They'd only stop him if he took a plane to someplace other than Los Angeles, if he bought a ticket to South America. If he left Puerto Vallarta two days early, then wouldn't the Pasadena Police, and Susan Avery, assume he was feeling the pressure and close in on him? Better to stay, better to pretend nothing was wrong. Suppose they arrested him in Los Angeles when he got off the plane. Why did you leave Mexico the day after you got there? If he said he had a meeting, Avery would check, and they'd want to know why he'd lied.

Now I must pretend to be a happy tourist, the happy lover, he thought. The weekend disappeared in this act. After breakfast they took a boat to a pretty little bay a few hours south of Puerto Vallarta. If they had been followed by the police, Griffin couldn't recognize the tail. There was a band on the boat, and Mexican couples danced while American tourists sat on the upper decks, overdosing on tequila and Corona beer. June tugged Griffin's hand and dragged him to the dance floor. She bought him two shots of tequila and forced him to move to the music. He loved her for letting him get lost in the crowd. He danced, and he was happy to dance. Chubby Mexican women in thick-soled, high-heeled sandals danced closely with their men. Children were dancing too. Americans watched and Mexicans danced, and now Griffin danced, badly, he knew, all that the liquor did was coax him to the floor, but it didn't matter if he had no rhythm, he was moving. He kissed June and he was happy. He would remember this day when he was in jail.

When they came back to the hotel in the late afternoon, they showered and then lay on the bed, ready to make love. They were both tired. They slept.

Griffin woke up first. It was dark, almost ten o'clock. June sat up and watched him as he moved from the bed and walked to the balcony. The policeman was in the garden again.

There was no point in pretending that he didn't see the man, thought Griffin, since it was impossible to ignore him; it was better to let him know that this gringo does not look rudely through Mexicans as though they're invisible. The policeman looked up at Griffin. Griffin nodded at him. The Mexican tilted his head, the contact was reassuring, promising easy treatment if there were an arrest.

"I love you," said June, leaving the bed. Again she hugged him from behind and rested her chin on his shoulder. She said it again. "I love you."

Griffin wondered how much the policeman knew. Had he been told simply to watch this couple and to report quickly if they snuck away to the airport? Or did he look at this couple on the balcony and see two killers?

And what should he say to June? He held her hand where she hugged his chest. He squeezed her fingers, hoping this would feel to her like a love he wasn't yet ready to declare. She kissed his ear.

"So?" she said.

"I love you too. I do." The policeman lit a cigarette. Did June include him in the romance of the place? Did she even see him?

"You're one of the best men I've ever met in my life."

"You've got me all wrong."

"I don't know what I would have done without you after David was killed."

"All I did was offer a little sympathy."

"Sometimes I think about the night David died, the night you called him. What if it had been you who had died that night, if you'd been mugged."

"I parked on the street."

"But if you hadn't. If you'd parked behind the theater, the killer could have found you instead of David. It could have happened that way."

"I suppose. Or to someone else. David could have come home, I could have come home."

"But say you had been killed; you didn't have to go to David's funeral, but you did. I know I wouldn't have gone to your funeral, not after one phone call. And I think I would have felt awful, somewhere in my, I don't know, my heart, my soul, I would have thought, whoa, if I hadn't told him that David was in Pasadena, he wouldn't have gone there and been killed."

"Well, you would have been the instrument of my fate, and that's out of your control."

"But the thing is, you didn't have to extend yourself and you did. And I respected you for it, I really did."

"There's a long road from respect to love."

"Well, you're cute and you're rich. That doesn't hurt."

"I thought I was fat."

"So am I." She kissed his ear again. The policeman walked away, toward the hotel's large bar.

"Were you in love with David?"

"Yes."

"Then maybe it's a little soon for you to be in love with me."

"I know, but it's how I feel, and I don't care what anyone thinks."

"I'm not talking about other people, I'm talking about how it's difficult to know your feelings when you've been through something awful. Everything gets confused."

"But you haven't been through anything like I have, and you just said you love me. So what do we do about that?"

"We just have to be careful." I am a monster, he thought. I am the worst person who ever lived.

When they made love this time, he controlled her completely, every flutter, every change in her pulse. He could guide her pleasure with the softest imaginable touch; it was his magnetic field drawing a brush against hers, to catch the smallest impulse at the tip of a finger and return it to her, build the pressure, and then let it out. Her breath was the meter. She wanted to do him, but he wouldn't let her, and this increased her desire and he still said no.

"Why?" she asked him. She was sweating, damp hair stuck to her forehead, hiding her glazed eyes.

"Not yet," was all he said, holding out hope like a drug.

He thought of Bonnie Sherow. Would she think he was the devil for making such brilliant love to the woman he had widowed? And it was brilliant. How could it not be, if this was the last weekend he'd spend with a woman? Had a man ever been so selfless with a woman? Of course she loved him; who had ever been so generous? He wondered if he was making love like a woman. He could do things with his fingers, give each one a personality of its own, send a squadron of lovers to June. June understood momentum, she knew how to be slow. Bonnie always seemed to be somewhere else. Why did he still care about her, think about her?

Sunday they stayed at the hotel and ate a large breakfast from a buffet in the dining room. They ate papaya with lime, eggs with Mexican sausage, beans, toasted rolls, drank coffee mixed with chocolate and cinnamon. They went to the beach and rubbed lotion on each other and rented an umbrella and slept. The police came by a few times, but Griffin didn't care about them anymore. He was in a cage, with an entrance in California, and the Mexican police couldn't touch him, they could only observe. Let them, he thought.

They ordered lunch on the beach, soft, rolled tacos filled with broiled fish and avocado and lime. After a nap they went for a swim. They were in the water for an hour and a half, floating on their backs and bumping their legs together, paddling between buoys.

"What was the idea?" she asked him.

"What idea?"

"The idea you wanted to talk about with David."

Was this the first volley of the interrogation? Had Susan Avery coached her? He could tell her he'd forgotten, but no one would believe that. "I wanted to talk about his Japan story."

"I always liked that one," she said. "I wish he'd written it."

"Yes." What else could he say?

They were both silent for a few minutes. A sailboat was close to the shore, and the people on board waved to them. June floated on her back and watched a tourist wearing a parachute tied to a speedboat get pulled around the bay, a few stories above the water.

"I don't think I've ever been this relaxed," said June. "And I bet you haven't, either."

"Probably not."

"How long will it last?"

"We leave in the morning."

"No, I meant, how long before we lose this feeling?"

"As long as the tan lasts."

"Can I ask you a question?"

"Of course."

"How come you don't have a girlfriend?"

"I do, sort of." He wanted to tell June some kind of truth.

"The one who couldn't go to the ball."

"Yes."

"Does she know you're here with me?"

"No."

"Where is she?"

"In Los Angeles."

"Why aren't you with her?"

"I told her I was busy. We're not as close as we used to be."

"Will you see her Monday night?"

"I don't think so. We keep making plans, but we never seem to get together."

"So she's not really your girlfriend."

"Her friends would say I am. I suppose my friends would say the same thing."

"Will you tell her about this weekend?"

"I don't know."

"Why not?"

"I don't know."

"It doesn't sound like she's really your girlfriend. You don't love her, do you?"

"I thought I told you that I love *you*."

"Men say lots of things they don't really mean."

"I meant it at the time."

"Yes, that's one of the things you hear men say, they say that one a lot."

"I don't love her."

"Have you told her that you do?"

"Not in a while."

"Has she told you that she loves you?"

"I don't think so."

"That's impossible. You don't forget someone telling you that she loves you."

"Yes, she once told me that she loved me. But we broke up after that. We've been speaking again."

"But now you've met me."

"Yes." He thought of a few questions he could ask. What did she expect? And why wasn't June married to Kahane? Was there a match between Griffin and June worth pursuing, because both had been wary of marriage? Were both of them the kind that didn't trust? Weren't her questions too pointed, wasn't she taking something out on him? Would she prefer that he had lied? Or did some cell in her body know that he had killed Kahane; was she examining him in preparation for his trial? That was not a question he would ask. But the others, if he asked them, he would be saying, Good, let's clear the air, let's see how well we fight, let's test this love. Maybe it was better to give her the lead. It was the least he could do.

He had to say something. "I think you're disappointed with me because I'm not the saint you thought I was, because I kept something from you, or because I didn't tell an old girlfriend that I'd be in Mexico with another woman. I'm just a guy. Maybe I have a big office and a fancy car, and I know how to wear a tuxedo and call for a limousine, so it looks like I have my life together, but love confuses everyone. I'm no exception."

They had drifted a mile down the beach. June splashed the water aimlessly, like a bored kid waiting to be told to stop splashing. Had he chastised her? That was not his intent. She had been mad at him for concealing Bonnie from her, and her from Bonnie, and instead of fueling the anger, he had once more made himself the hero of reason. She swam to him and with strong arms pushed him backward, daring him to resist. Then she growled at him, because she was frustrated with him, with life, with her grief, and because she loved him, and then she kissed him.

"Let's go in," she said, leading him to the shore.

That night they went to bed, and again he played her with his hands. She reached for him, but he wouldn't do what she wanted. This time she didn't ask why.

When they checked out of the hotel in the morning, June did not know that the police car following them from the hotel to the airport was their official escort. After they cleared customs, the police waited with them in the lounge. Griffin led them to the duty-free shop, where he bought June some perfume, her favorite, Karl Lagerfeld. He wondered if he should buy some for Bonnie, but June stayed by his side. He could always get some at a department store. He could go from one to the other if they wore the same scent.

Then they were on the plane, and then they were back in Los Angeles.

CHAPTER SEVENTEEN

If Susan Avery or anyone else from the Pasadena Police Department watched their arrival in Los Angeles, they were invisible to Griffin. He missed the Mexican police. He should have said good-bye to them. Would they be told when he was arrested, sent a formal letter thanking them for their cooperation? Griffin idly wondered if the State Department involved itself in every international manhunt. Then he wondered why it mattered to him, and he knew it was because he wanted to feel important.

A limousine driver holding a cardboard sign that read MILL took their bags after they left the terminal.

As soon as they were in the car, Griffin called Jan. "I'm back," he said.

"How was Mexico?" she asked.

"Did Dick Mellen call?"

"Yes, and your old friend Susan Avery. She wants you to call her immediately. I asked if they had a break in the case, and she said she was superstitious and didn't want to jinx anything."

Griffin didn't want to call Susan Avery with June in the car. "If she calls back, tell her I'll call her when I'm in the office. I should be there in forty-five minutes."

He called his lawyer. His secretary put him through after it took her just enough time to interrupt another call with Griffin's name.

"Mr. Griffin Mill," said Dick Mellen, who didn't want to contain his happiness at bearing some kind of good news.

"What's the word?" asked Griffin, playing along with him.

"How'd you like to run a production company?"

"A studio?"

"No. An office, a few assistants, someone to handle business affairs, and sixty million dollars to play with."

"That's all? How many movies can you make for sixty million dollars?"

"You can make four or five a year."

"And who's the distributor?"

"Tri-Star or MGM. That hasn't been worked out."

"I don't think so, I don't know. Let me think about it. How much will they pay me?"

"That's the good news. They want you. And for the next two years they'll pay you eight hundred thousand, plus stock, plus a piece of each picture. They know all about you. They like you. You'll like them."

"Let me think about it."

"They want to know by tomorrow. Someone else is interested, but your name came up and they asked me if you were available. I would have said no two weeks ago, but Larry Levy is no one to laugh at. To be honest with you, there's a cloud over you at the studio right now."

"And your friends still want me?"

"And my friends still want you."

"You think I should take this job?"

"It's a risk. You can fail. It might be hard to get back to a big job with a major studio if you bomb. But you're not going to bomb, you're going to be a massive success, and you'll make a lot of money and have a lot of fun."

They said good-bye.

"Good news?" asked June.

"I don't know. I've been on a certain track for a while, and someone is offering me a chance to get off it, but it's not the most prestigious job in town. People will think I've been demoted if I take it. It's a small production company looking for a leader."

"That's exciting."

"I once turned down an offer to run Columbia for a million dollars a year."

"Why?"

"I wanted to run the company I work for."

"But Levison runs the company you work for."

"Yeah, well, I thought he was leaving."

They were driving up Outpost; her house was around the next two curves.

"It was a great weekend," she said. "It was too short."

After a subdued last kiss they shook hands. She tapped him on the arm with a fist. "Thank you," she said. The driver carried her bags to her house, and she waved from the door after she opened it. Maybe she won't be arrested right away, he thought.

He called Susan Avery as the car drove toward Burbank. She answered the phone.

"You called?" he said. Of course, she'd been following the news from the Mexican police; she probably knew about the hug on the balcony and the kiss in the ocean.

"Hello, Griffin, how are you?" She was too friendly, and he knew he was in the snare of technique.

"Wonderful. I just got back from a weekend in Mexico. I should have stayed a month."

"Why didn't you?"

"I'm always afraid if I'm gone too long, they'll change the lock on my office."

"Where were you?"

"Puerto Vallarta."

"Oh, that's nice."

"Susan, what's up?"

"Well, Griffin, I know we've taken a lot of your time already, and I promise you that after this last request I don't think we'll need to bother you again."

"Has there been a break in the case?"

"We don't know. Listen, Griffin, this is sort of difficult for me because I like you, but I was wondering if maybe you'd get in touch with a lawyer today and both of you come down to the station. You can come alone, but as a friend, I'm telling you, bring a lawyer."

"Is somebody accusing me of the murder?" Better to take this head-on, not act as though I don't know what's coming.

"I told the captain that you'd come without a subpoena, but if you want to be served while you're at the studio, be my guest."

"I'll be there in half an hour." He hung up. He told the limousine driver to stay on the long boulevard that passed the studio and follow it all the way to Pasadena.

If he didn't call a lawyer, wouldn't he look like the guilty person trying to look innocent? But he was scared of calling a lawyer. To get a criminal lawyer he'd have to go through Mellen, whose motto was: "Trust everybody, trust nobody." Griffin didn't want Hollywood to know he'd been suspected of a murder if he wasn't arrested. And there was still some hope. But he needed a lawyer; obviously there was a witness, or a fingerprint, something real. He called Mellen. His secretary said he was in a meeting.

"Look, I need some help on something right away, we're stuck on a story problem. Who does he recommend for criminal work?"

"Phil Brophy."

"Good, what's his number?"

She gave it to him. Griffin called him. He used Mellen's name with the secretary and said it was an emergency. She told him Brophy was in court. Griffin asked to speak to another lawyer, anyone. She put him through to Jeff Beckett. Beckett had a clear, high voice.

"My name is Griffin Mill. I'm a client of Richard Mellen at Mellen, Ottoway and Green."

"Aha. So you're in show business."

"Very much so. Mr. Beckett, I'm not quite sure what's going on, but I've been asked to bring a lawyer with me to the Pasadena police station. I'll explain it in person. I need some help immediately, and I can pay any fee."

"Have you been arrested?"

"No, but I'm being subpoenaed."

"What's the charge?"

"Can you come?"

"I'll be there in an hour."

Yes, at this point even an innocent man would bring an expensive lawyer to the station to intimidate the police.

When the limousine pulled into the station parking lot, Griffin told the driver that he wanted to wait a while. The car phone rang. It was Levison.

"Where are you?"

"I'm stuck in traffic."

"You're missing a staff meeting."

"Just a second. You gave me permission to take a vacation."

"Yes, but you were supposed to be back this morning."

"I'll be back this afternoon."

"This is quite annoying."

Griffin hung up. The driver knocked on the glass partition. Griffin lowered it.

"Do you know how long we're going to be here? I have to call the office. I'm supposed to make a pickup in Beverly Hills in twenty-five minutes. I'm going to be late."

"I'm sorry. I'll be here for a while. This is a really stupid thing, but the company I lease my car from is charging me with theft."

"Why?"

"Because they're assholes, that's why. Because they wouldn't give me a new car when mine kept breaking down, and they wouldn't do repairs, and I finally stopped sending them money."

"What kind of car?"

"Guess."

"Porsche."

"You got it."

"Why don't you pay?"

"That's what I'll probably do right now. I'll fight for my principles, but hey, I don't want to get booked and fingerprinted over this, you know what I mean? It's not the battle of my life."

"I hear you," said the driver.

"Time to go in," said Griffin.

"Let me just call the office," said the driver. The office told him to stay with Griffin.

As Griffin opened the door, the driver rushed to open it for him. Griffin told him not to, and the driver understood that Griffin didn't want to make a display of himself in a police-station parking lot, or any more of a display than the limousine presented.

Susan Avery met him in the lobby. "I appreciate this," she said. What if she knew everything? he wondered. What if she knew about the postcards and why I really killed Kahane? Would she treat me with caution, knowing that I'd probably get off on a defense of insanity? Should I start acting insane?

"My lawyer is on his way. I thought it would be best to have one here. I don't know what you're cooking up, but this is a hell of a way to do business."

"Business?"

"Everything is business."

"We want you to take part in a lineup."

"I told you, I didn't see anyone." This was a mistake, he shouldn't have been flip.

"Griffin, we want you to be *in* the lineup."

"Not until my lawyer arrives." This was not time to say something easy, like, "Give me a break."

She brought Griffin to a waiting room. Jeff Beckett came in half an hour later. He was in his forties, with curly dark hair. He leaned forward as he walked, and he had a strong handshake. Griffin supposed he played squash. You could see the eager high-school boy, the debate-team champ, the mother's hero. Griffin liked him.

"So, what do they want you for?" he asked.

"I think they want me for murder."

"How come they haven't arrested you yet?"

"Don't you want to know if I'm guilty?"

"That's up to a jury, and I wouldn't ask you in here, anyway." He indicated the room with his hand.

"They want me to be in a lineup. I was one of the last people to see someone before he was murdered. About a month ago. It was in Pasadena. I barely knew the guy."

"I can't really keep you out of a lineup without making a big stink, and that never looks good."

"But what if the witness thinks I'm the one? What if I'm picked?"

"Then I guess you get arrested. We'll bail you out and fight like hell."

Griffin was silent.

"Look," said Beckett, "this is serious stuff, and it has to follow a certain procedure. I'll be with you all the way."

They left the room. Susan Avery met them in the hall. She took Griffin up a flight of stairs, around a few corners, and down another staircase. She opened a door and let him into a small room with five men. Griffin recognized one as a policeman he'd seen at the station when he first visited. He didn't know the others. Three were Griffin's general size and color, a little overweight, light brown hair. Of the others, one was taller, two were shorter, one of them was fat.

A policeman assigned them numbers and stood them in a line. Then he opened a door, and they were led into a small space with a floor-to-ceiling mirror on one side, and a wall with horizontal stripes to measure their height. They were told to face forward. Beyond the mirror, someone studied them. Susan Avery was there. The room was soundproof; if the witness was talking, he couldn't hear her. He didn't know why, but he assumed the witness was a woman.

Each of the men was told to step forward and then to turn from side to side. Griffin was number two. He took a step forward as he imagined a cop would who was doing a job, with a sure motion, hinting of the military. The real cop was next to him and stepped forward slowly. Was he pretending to be guilty?

Griffin was singled out again. So was number one, who was taller than him.

After ten minutes they were brought back to the holding room. They waited there for twenty minutes. Griffin wanted to get a message to the limousine driver, to open the suitcase in the trunk and bring him his toothbrush and razor, but of course they wouldn't let him keep the razor. He could ask for some clean underwear from the suitcase.

Susan Avery came into the room and thanked everyone. Jeff Beckett was behind her.

"That's it?" asked Griffin.

"That's all she wrote," she said.

"Did they pick anyone?"

"They didn't pick you."

"I was thinking, you know, I was on the street when he was killed. And a witness to the murder might have seen me there and, in the lineup, would have remembered my face."

"There you go with my defense," said Beckett.

Griffin couldn't believe that it was over. They were joking now, but it seemed that Avery had only followed a lead, because yes, someone had seen the murder, but it was dark, and Griffin had been impossible to identify. Avery never seriously believed that Griffin killed Kahane, she was only doing her job.

"What do you do now?" asked Griffin.

"I just have to ask you a few more questions," she said.

"With my lawyer in the room."

"With your lawyer in the room."

"Go ahead."

"How long have you known June Mercator?"

"Since Kahane's funeral."

"You'd never met her before that."

"No."

"How well did you know Kahane?"

"I really didn't. Not at all."

"Thank you, Griffin. I'm sorry if we've inconvenienced you."

"If you catch the killer, let me know." They shook hands warmly, and Griffin walked with Jeff Beckett into the sunshine.

"So, Counselor, how much did that cost me?"

"Two hundred and fifty dollars."

"Step into my office." He brought the lawyer to the limousine. He took his traveler's checks from his wallet. There were four hundreds.

"Do you have fifty?" asked Griffin. He signed three checks. The lawyer gave him three twenties. Griffin gave him two fives in return. They were even.

"She thinks you're guilty," said Beckett. "I think she thinks you just got away with murder."

"That's her problem," said Griffin. It was a little lame, but he couldn't think of anything to say that would make himself look innocent. He supposed it didn't matter. He knew her suspicion lingered because of his stupid monologue to the cop who followed him in the Beverly Hilton.

"Say hello to Dick Mellen," said Beckett.

Griffin put a finger to his lips, meaning silence. Beckett understood. The driver asked Griffin how things had turned out.

"I settled."

"Good," said the driver. "You want to go back to the office?"

"No," said Griffin. "Take me home. Beverly Glen."

As the limousine drove through Pasadena, Griffin called Dick Mellen.

"Yes," said Griffin. "I'm interested in the job. Set up the meeting."

"You won't regret it."

"You can't say that," snapped Griffin.

"Then I won't," said Mellen.

"It's a big move," said Griffin.

"Well, you can have your doubts, and I understand them, but I think you'll be pleasantly surprised. These people want to back your taste, your vision."

Griffin leaned back into the seat. He was smiling. He could feel the smile, the rare, spontaneous, beautiful smile. He was at one with the world around him, and he let the tension leave him, just pack its bags and walk away from him.

He would call in sick today, and if Levison was angry with him, so what? He didn't care if he never saw the man again, or his office, or the studio. Let them lock me out, he thought. Why bother with Larry Levy and Oakley and Civella, why put up with that anymore? The chances were slim he'd be head of production; Levy would probably get the job, and Griffin felt, to his core, that now he didn't want the job anymore. Mellen was right to have found him this new company. He was still young, he was strong, and he welcomed the challenge.

EPILOGUE

Six months passed. He marked the time not from the lineup, or the day he had left the studio, but from the Writer's last contact with him, the phone call. So much had happened, and so quickly, that days would go by without his giving the Writer a thought.

Jan had followed him to the new job. He had weighed the problems of keeping her—that she knew him too well, that she was there during the postcards, the first days of Larry Levy and the killing of David Kahane—against the problem of training someone new, and he decided that he didn't have the time.

She included the square red envelope with the Seattle postmark with his mail. The word PERSONAL was typed across the the bottom. Inside the envelope was a greeting card, with a sentimental photograph of a beach at sunset. Tucked inside was a thousand dollars in cash. And a letter, folded in half and then folded again:

> Dear Griffin,
>
> As you can see, I'm out of town now, and I plan to stay here for a long time, probably forever. It's better this way. I wasn't sure how I'd feel, whether I'd miss Los Angeles, miss the movie business, and hate myself for quitting, but it hasn't been like that at all. Well, it's hard for me to see movies if I know the writers, but actually, I knew so few who ever saw their screenplays produced that it's not a problem. And I had trouble seeing them when I was in town! Anyway, I decided to leave the day a friend of mine, one of the lucky ones, told me this story. It's not really a story, it's just a picture, an image.

He was working one Sunday afternoon with a producer at the producer's house in Malibu. The producer's father is really rich—that's part of the story. They were working on a script. At the end of the day a movie star, I won't tell you who—oh, what the hell, it was Arnold Schwarzenegger—came over. He was there to have dinner. My friend wasn't invited, didn't expect it, that's not an issue here, anyway. Schwarzenegger looked great, smoked the stub of a fat cigar and asked some really intelligent questions about the script they were working on. My friend was impressed. I found myself trying to tear everyone down as the story was being told, trying to make them less. For example: When my friend described the house, I said, "Oh, it's his father's house," and my friend said, "No, it's his." "His father bought it for him," I said, and my friend said, "Yeah, so what?" And that really stopped me. "Yeah, so what?" The producer was enjoying his life, he was having fun, he wasn't confused, he didn't hate himself. And I thought, Why am I torturing this executive? This is the sickest thing I've ever heard of. Why am I jealous of a rich kid whose father bought him a three-million-dollar playpen? My father's helped me out, and that's an advantage over someone who's had to make every dime himself. So I didn't get a movie made. So what?

Oh, the money . . . for the windshields. Sorry.

So the Writer had quit Hollywood. He had thought about his threats and awakened from his delirium of hatred. Griffin was happy for him. So few who should, ever leave. He crumpled the envelope and tucked the cash, the card, and the letter into a pocket.

He wondered what the Writer was doing now. Working in a bookstore? Had he returned to a family business? Was he a professor or a high-school teacher? And was he really so casual about his failure to see his vision on the screen? Would he ever write another script? If he did, would he submit it here? Griffin looked out his window at Century City. The Writer had kept track of Griffin's career, knew about his new job, knew that Levison was out and that Levy now ran the studio. The Writer couldn't know that Griffin and Levy were friends now, since Griffin had left the studio before a battle with Levy and there was no reason to quarrel. Would the Writer understand that Griffin loved his new job, loved working in Century City? There he could concentrate on getting movies made, and one was already in production, with another ready to go in a few weeks. It was an exciting time for him.

Griffin left the office that evening and drove home through Beverly Hills. He had a thousand dollars in his pocket, and he wanted to buy something for his wife. The stores were closed. Tomorrow he would come back and buy her a pearl necklace. Or should he give the money away, hand it to a homeless family camped in a city parking lot?

As he turned into the driveway, he checked the rearview mirror. No one was following him. He took the cash from his pocket and slipped it inside the glove compartment. If they went out to dinner that night and were stopped for speeding, he would have to produce his registration and proof of insurance, and his wife might see the thousand dollars. He locked the compartment and decided that if they did go out, they would take her car; they would take the Saab.